To Do[...]

With love from
 Catherine Orchard

SPIRIT OF DREAMS

Catherine Orchard

MINERVA PRESS
ATLANTA LONDON SYDNEY

SPIRIT OF DREAMS
Copyright © Catherine Orchard 1999

All Rights Reserved

No part of this book may be reproduced in any form
by photocopying or by any electronic or mechanical means,
including information storage or retrieval systems,
without permission in writing from both the copyright
owner and the publisher of this book.

ISBN 1 75410 752 3

First Published 1999 by
MINERVA PRESS
315–317 Regent Street
London W1R 7YB

Printed in Great Britain for Minerva Press

Spirit of Dreams

Preface

I dreamed a dream and it was so vivid, and to become so real, that I saw the dream unfolding in my life before my eyes. I felt compelled to write down the dream and the unfolding, lest it should fade like the rainbow. The purpose of the dream, and the action I must take, fell open before my eyes. When I opened my grandmother's Bible it was marked at St Matthew's Gospel, Chapter 24, Verse 14, 'And this Gospel of the Kingdom shall be preached in all the world for a witness unto all nations.'

I would like to acknowledge and thank all the people mentioned in this journal for the vital part they played. I would also like to thank those who typed, proof-read and made possible the publishing of this book.

This book has been written as events happened, in the form of a journal, and I hope you enjoy my sharing with you in what I can only describe as an amazing experience... in bearing witness to the power of the Holy Spirit.

St Columba copied Finian's Bible, a book described as, like an angel with pictures, and letters in gold and red and green and blue. This is how I pictured my journal – reflecting the beauty of the Celtic art, with swirls and scrolls and illuminated lettering.

Contents

Introduction		9
One	Diary of Iona	11
Two	A Vision	22
Three	Journey Back	40
Four	The Vision Unfolds	52
Five	Healing	63
Six	You shall not be Overcome	76
Seven	Farewell to Summer	85
Eight	Two Angels	90
Nine	Pilgrimage Continued	97
Ten	The Gift of Sight	102
Eleven	The Shortest Day	107
Twelve	Adieu! And Forward to the Dawn	110
Notes to the Text		123

Introduction

I dreamed a dream that I was in Jerusalem travelling along the old dusty road to Jerricho, and that dream came true at Easter in 1994. I dreamed a dream of travelling through the mountains and highlands of Scotland, and sailing the seas to Iona, and that dream came true in April 1997.

In 1997 I was to go on a pilgrimage. Five years ago I went on a pilgrimage to Israel and followed Jesus round Galilee and up the Mount of Olives to Jerusalem – I will never forget the Golden Dome and shimmering spires floating in the clouds, and I realised in the Temple (Dominus Flevit) how Jesus felt as he wept over the fate of Jerusalem and the world.

I was to go on a pilgrimage to Iona during Easter, but such a large group from the Churches in Hazel Grove could not be accommodated, so I discounted this until I heard I would be going on the 19th of April, and would I pay the deposit etc!

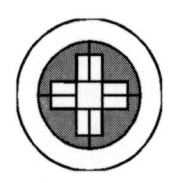

Chapter One
Diary of Iona

The sky in Iona was deep blue and the sea was a pure blue and calm. There was a presence in Iona and a sure spiritual belonging. The abbey and the chapel bridged the centuries. What was here had nothing to do with time – the abbey that St Columba founded in AD 563 was filled with the same Holy Spirit, and the presence of God watched over the same struggle of man to seek the truth. Here was a place where pilgrims might struggle against the elements and get ravaged and scarred in the battles of life, but above the turmoil of wind and rain, as we went round the island on our pilgrimage, was a peace and a sureness that God was in control.

From the moment I left the ferry, eager to reach the abbey, I was to follow a spiritual path, as direct as the path from the sea to our destination.

My room was in the Abbot's house a few yards from a field with new-born lambs and an ancient stone arch – the only remains of a once solid stone building. I was quite a way from the accommodation in the abbey – having to go down steps, along the cloisters, and past the reception porch through a huge oak door and out into the open. I then walked past a small garden of peace with white doves and on to a gravel path that led round a building to reach the Abbot's house. I found a short cut – across a gravel yard into the common room through a French window – into the abbey and our place of meeting. This little journey was in pitch darkness, at night, with only the stars or moon as light. We were all given duties at breakfast the next day. Mine was to sweep and mop, with an old wringing mop and metal bucket, a stone stairway and corridor leading to the common room and the cloisters. I shared this task with Mavis. Mavis and I used to wander down the 'Valley' twenty-five years ago – strange we should be together in Iona? Not strange to God though! After Communion at 10.15 a.m. we shared a little piece of our Communion oat cake with a stranger as we left the chapel and joined the outside world. On the evening of this Sunday we watched a video of MacLeod and the Queen, and saw how the abbey was being rebuilt from the ruins. We returned to the abbey chapel at 9 p.m. for a quiet Quaker service.

Prayers were said and I thanked God for children and that they might know of his love for them. I thought of our family, Peter, Ros and the children, Iona and Ellie, and how lucky we were to have the children with us. Perhaps it was not 'lucky' to God! Lucky also to have our Canadian friends. The bell rang on Monday at 7.45 a.m. and we had breakfast at 8.15 a.m. Porridge, healthy brown bread and various spreads.

The Service for Monday followed:

> Morning opens wide before us like a door into the light.
> Just beyond, the day lies waiting,
> Ready to throw off the night.
> And we stand upon its threshold
> Poised to turn and take its flight.[1]

At 10 a.m. Martin gathered us together for meditation. We were asked to write the names of five people – past or present – who had helped us on our pilgrimage. Out of the five we were then asked to concentrate on one and have a conversation with this person, and jot down our thoughts. To my surprise, I focused on William Wordsworth and found certain facts in his life were very similar to my own. We both lost our parents – especially mother early in life – we were both particularly close to a sister and we both went in the wrong direction, depressed by what we saw and recovered through poetry, which led to a deeper faith! I quoted:

> My heart leaps up when I behold a rainbow in the sky,
> so it was when I was a child,
> so it is now I am a man,
> so be it when I grow old, or let me die.
> The child is father of the man
> And I could wish my days to be,
> Bound each to each in natural piety. [2]

I did not see a rainbow whilst I was on Iona, but as we travelled home on the coach someone shouted, 'Jackie look!' And sure enough, a complete arc of colours went over our heads… and our hearts leapt up.

After coffee we went into a quiet room for 'Stories' told by Ron. 'The boy and the dog'; 'Milk for the Cat'; 'Lullaby Story'; and best of all, 'Malachai' – and how he wanted to dance at his daughter's wedding. We then had a light lunch. I wrote a postcard home – showing the abbey and Bishop's house.

We walked to the beach and collected pebbles. It was windy and we stopped to admire the highland cattle and new-born lambs. It was my turn to serve and set tables so I hurried back. After the evening meal we went to the chapel for a 'Peace and Justice Service'.

As we went in we were given red poppies. During the service the young ones brought in banners declaring their concerns on land mines. After carrying the banners aloft they placed a basket near each banner. They then invited us to go forward and leave our poppy in the basket, upon which we felt compelled to act, having read the banners carefully. As we left we collected our poppy, determined to pray for the cause we had chosen.

Not long after we returned home, Princess Diana was on the news campaigning for the end to land mines. This became a real issue for the government who, where we supplied land mines, acted on this dreadful situation.

At 10 p.m. we joined in a 'Cellidh' – 'Yellow Submarine', 'Sky Boat Song', 'Streets of London' were among some of the songs we sang. Also, a strange song of 'Butties flying through the air', called 'Jeelies'. It made us all laugh even though we did not understand a word – perhaps God did!
Tuesday, and breakfast of porridge and nice bread and spreads. Followed by the Service for Tuesday.

> Today I awake and God is before me.
> At night as I dreamt, he summoned the day;
> For God never sleeps,
> But patterns the morning, with slithers of gold, or glory in grey.
> Today I affirm, the Spirit within me
> At worship and work in struggle and rest
> The Spirit inspires, all life which is changing.
> From fearing to faith, from broken to blest.
> Today I arise and Christ is beside me.
> He walked through the dark, to scatter new light.
> Yes, Christ is alive, and beckons his people.
> To hope and to heal, resist and invite.
> Today I enjoy The Trinity round me.
> Above and beneath, before and behind.
> The maker, the Son, The Spirit together.
> They called me to life, and call me their friend.

'They call me to life' – The Holy Spirit was to come to me, but not yet, and I was unaware. All I knew was that I was waiting on God, I was expecting. We returned to the abbey, and Mavis and I tackled our stone steps with enthusiasm and enjoyed each other's company as we used to all those years ago when we walked together down the 'Valley'.

We completed our tasks and gathered in a quiet room for meditation. In the middle of the room was a huge lump of clay – brown earthy clay! We were invited to take a lump of clay and a board, and plenty of newspaper to protect our laps and the carpet. I tugged a sizeable lump from the mound of clay, and it stained my hands brown and went deep into my nails. There was industrious silence as we worked silently to make a form and some sense out of this dirty lump. I found I was recreating the scene from the window – where in the distance, mountains folded backwards from the sea increasing in height, and yet decreasing in clarity. I started to form a few hill shapes and then these increased in size until at the front of my board were huge peaks of clay. I enjoyed doing this – it did not require any great skill or fiddly concentration, but I felt a solid creative satisfaction.

Perhaps that is how God felt when he created the real scene from the window? I asked myself where was Christ in my scene, and I took a small piece of clay and formed a Celtic cross, which I put at the front of my board where the largest mountains were. And now for us the people, where were we? I rolled some small heads and stuck them on stumps and placed them at the back of the board, furthest from the cross. We had some easy hills to climb first, but would we be able to climb the mountains? Did we have any idea how hard the journey was that lay ahead? This was Tuesday and the sky was blue and the sea was blue. It seemed easy to be a pilgrim here on Iona. Tomorrow we would walk round the island on a pilgrimage, stopping to pray at places of historical and religious significance.

After coffee we had a talk on Celtic Spirituality. Two words emerged with prominence – pilgrimage and presence. I, like every visitor to Iona, felt the presence of the Saints here – in the buildings, especially St Columba's chapel; in the old Celtic crosses; in every arch and stone, in the mounds of earth constructed to protect the buildings from wind and storm. The presence of God in the creation of Iona, the mountains, the sea, the sky.

After lunch we boarded a small boat and set off for Staffa. The sea was deep blue and perfectly calm. We sat back in the sunshine and enjoyed the short trip to the island. The sailor in charge of the boat explained to me that there was an easterly wind and this meant the sea was calm. 'But it is changing,' he said. 'When the wind blows from the west, that is when the sea is rough, and then landing on Staffa is impossible.' However, we 'landed'. I found I was clutching Iona's hand and together we jumped from boat to a rocky outcrop.

There was no proper landing stage, and as the boat seemed to surge and swell – one minute alongside the rocks and the next a deep fathom away – it was a heart-stopping jump. We started up some steep metal steps, higher and higher, no turning back, with only enough room for one pair of feet on each rung. I went first, still clutching tightly on to Iona's hand as she followed. We found ourselves on top of the world, and set off to explore. Gradually the rest of the party went their individual ways and we seemed to be the only two left. We cautiously looked for puffins, realising that the next step could be a deep ravine.

Fortunately we found a grassy patch of daisies and rested – recovered from our ordeal – and made some daisy chains. We enjoyed our simple company and the total freedom from cares. I thought back to how we had set out from Hazel Grove early in the morning, and as I climbed the steps of the coach, how a voice had called me and Iona begged me to sit with her.

We seemed to be good friends on the basis of one short meeting – which I found difficult to recall – and when we had paid our various monies for the ferries, coach etc. And here we were on top of the world, without a care in the world – all part of God's plan.

In the distance we saw a figure coming towards us carrying a small child – we soon recognised Peter and Ellie. Peter sat down and asked me to hold Ellie while he drank some peppermint tea from a flask. We both agreed it was a difficult place to watch over such young and lively children. After Peter was refreshed I decided to have a drink, and holding our charges tightly we set off, picking our way carefully to the steps, then down, down to the rocks and boat. The sailor made a bit of a detour round the island and there were the puffins – we had seen them!

I was excused table laying duties, or rather had exchanged these duties so I could go over to the MacLeod Centre for dinner. Mushrooms, pasta, salad and a very successful chocolate mousse which the young ones soon polished off! This Tuesday evening we gathered for a talk by a Roman Catholic on Healing. She was very spiritual and had a calmness that I often see in Roman Catholics. I was happily reminded that this visit to Iona was a joint one with the other churches in Hazel Grove. We are so enriched when we are together – the Holy Spirit lets us understand our differences and we can rejoice in Christ together. My first friend at school was a Jewish boy and as we stood in our classrooms, had the register called and were led out for assembly and worship, we never failed to glance at each other and wonder. At eleven years old, another best friend went to the convent school, and our friendship ended. (Neither joined in our assembly).

Healing is vital. Illness and sin are locked together. However, a physical cure is not necessarily healing. Jesus's ministry started with healing – we must heal before we can struggle through the mountains and reach the cross. Jesus healed in different ways, and different conditions and sometimes healing was delayed in order that a greater healing could take place. Is it easier to say, 'Your sins are forgiven,' or 'Take up your bed and walk'?

At 9 p.m. there was to be a Healing Service. We were looking forward to this service very much, and I joined the others in the common room just before 9 p.m., eager to go to the chapel. Peter rushed into the common room and asked if anyone could baby-sit so Ros could go to the Healing Service. I had no hesitation in saying I would baby-sit – I felt this to be fulfilling – whether fulfilling for Peter and Ros, or for me, I did not know. I baby-sat so I did not go to the Healing Service, and although I asked – and it was obviously an important and moving service – I knew little of this service. This was to be a long evening and some of us went Scottish dancing until 11 p.m. and even discoing until midnight! The walk back to the abbey was relaxed and we chatted happily about the star formations, and Hale Bop – the comet that had been visible for ages as it spluttered and sparked across our night sky.

Wednesday and the day of our Pilgrimage – it was dark, wet and windy. What had happened to our blue sky? We enjoyed our Morning worship.

> Oh! the life of the world is a joy and a treasure,
> Unfolding in beauty the green growing tree,
> The changing of seasons in mountain and valley.
> The stars and the bright restless sea?[3]

Some of us had to rush back to the kitchens and make sandwiches for the Pilgrimage. I was in charge of the egg sandwiches and found it hard to resist eating a few! 10.15 a.m. and we set off – a bit unsure of the conditions but Peter our leader said that if we thought being a pilgrim was easy, it was certainly not! We set off round the island, stopping at the nunnery. This was a fascinating ruin of arches and rooms which gave a good feeling of what life was like for the nuns here. I returned and sat here several times, because there was a peace and an order that came like a glimpse into the past, and pervaded all things.

Our next stop was St Columba's Cove. We sheltered in the rocks, for a prayer, but the wind snatched the words away. When we emerged from the relative shelter of the rocks, and into the open bay, we were buffeted and clung to each other in order to stand our ground. We managed to pick up a pebble and throw it out to sea. To throw something away in our lives. I found this very hard – I could not think of anything of significance to throw away – but I enthusiastically gathered smooth green-veined pebbles to take back home. We were then due to go to a special place – Machair – for our sandwich lunch but Peter decided we needed to shelter, and he suggested we should go and shelter against a wall in the vicarage nearby. The van arrived with our sandwiches and urns of tea – what a wonderful sight! – and trays of crunch. It was a marvellous feast but reluctantly we had to return to the abbey owing to the weather. We were later told that this was the first time the Wednesday Pilgrimage had been abandoned since 1938! We were reluctant to change direction and head back to the abbey, even though it offered shelter, warmth and dry clothes. The wind disregarded our stubbornness, and as we turned to head back, it summoned a mighty strength and, blowing steadily against our backs, forced us at quite a pace to return swiftly from where we had so eagerly and hopefully set out. I hung my wet clothes and put my wet boots in one of the maze of rooms that went down under the abbey. The boiler and network of hot pipes ran along this labyrinth of airless, dark chambers making it ideal for drying. I went back to my room to examine my wave-worn pebbles.

> How sad a welcome! To each voyager
> Some ragged child holds up for sale a store of 'wave
>   worn' pebbles, pleading on the shore.
> Where once came monk and nun with gentle stir.
> Blessings to give, news ask, or suit prefer.[4]

William Wordsworth wrote this in 1833 whilst on a summer tour. He wrote this poem when he was sixty-three. His youthful inspiration, as he had recognised in his 'Ode to Immortality', had faded. He lived a comfortable life at Rydal Mount with no money worries. However, there are still glimpses of amazing beauty in his poetry.

No ragged child now, no monk, no nun. Plenty of 'wave worn' pebbles to give to the family and home group – blessings from Iona.

I not only had to set the tables and serve the meal but also to help clear away and wash up! I felt I deserved the luxury of listening to some more of Ron's stories: – 'The Giant' (the children and garden); 'Diane' (sick daughter, crumbs under the table for the dogs); 'Boaz' (who stole till Eli broke his back – and then let him down for Jesus to heal). Is it easier to say, 'Your sins are forgiven' or 'Take up your bed and walk'?

Wednesday finished with a service in the chapel and our Canadian friends – The Spirit Singers – sang in a special Choir Service for us. I returned to my tiny cell – the window was a slit and let in a tiny shaft of light but not enough for me to see where I had put anything. The bed fitted neatly along one wall, and there was just enough room for me to put my feet over the side of the bed in order to get up – if my shoe size had been larger than size five, I would have needed to walk like a crab to get to the door!

By the bed was a chest with a mirror above. The hanging space was to the right of the chest and consisted of four hooks on the wall. Then came the door. My suitcase stood in the only space left, under the four hooks. Next to my room on my right was a notice which said 'Staff', and a flight of stairs. On my left was another 'cell' and then a large room, where five Canadians slept. There was a lot of laughter and singing from this room, because as one of the Canadians explained, 'There are five of us in this room, and we are all single ladies, used to our own space!'

Opposite my room was a toilet and two hand bowls. The shower was to the right, with a large wooden door – leading outside – in between. So if you wanted to visit the toilet and bowl room and then go to the shower, it was likely that someone would blast through the wooden door, bumping into you and letting in a cold, fierce blast from outside.

Chapter Two
A Vision

Thursday got off to an excellent start – the deep blue sky had returned with its loyal echo spread out in the sea. The lambs were skipping and frolicking in the green tufts of grass, and had left the shelter of the stone wall, where they were all huddled during the previous day of storms. After breakfast we assembled in the chapel and sang, 'How lovely on the mountains are the feet of him who brings good news.' After the mopping duties we met for meditation. We read John 21 Verse 2 but I mainly focused on, 'Come Sacred Three my fortress be encircling me.' We turned in all directions and pointed as we said this.

Time for more stories! 'Monks and Rabbi in the garden'; 'Tabitha'; 'Stephen'; 'Good Samaritan'; and 'King in the Garden'. I liked the last one especially, and could vividly picture the King wandering about with weeds growing in his beard and crown askew!

Lunch was soup and solid brown bread. It gave us the energy and desire to walk round the island a bit. We visited the Parish Church, said a prayer inside, then sat on a bench for a while – still in prayer, keeping well to the Celtic tradition. We walked on and stopped when invited by the lapping waves and white sandy beach of a sheltered cove. We had been told that the sea was relatively warm because of the gulf stream, so we carefully placed our bare feet between the rocks and pebbles to reach the ebb and flow. What looked so welcoming was cold – absolutely cold. With completely numb feet I climbed back over some rocks, and discovered a rock pool several feet in depth and warm and clear. I called the others and we all splashed about like children. I then walked down to one of the few shops and bought some souvenirs – today was Thursday and the week was dwindling. For once I had not got any duties so I headed for the nunnery.

The nunnery consisted of quite extensive ruins – arches, steps, doorways, rooms with ledges and nooks and crannies. All open to the sky, so the blue and bright sunlight come flooding in. There is enough solid stonework remaining to show the life of obedience and security that belonged here. Two small birds singing their hearts out above an open arch near where I sat stretched their throats upwards and were at ease with my presence.

> And while upon the fancied scene
> I gazed with growing love, a higher power
> than fancy gave assurance of some work
> of glory thereforth with to be[5]

After our evening meal there was to be a concert of stories (Red Sea), jokes, songs, and even a sermon, rather a strange one from Peter.

We gathered in the chapel for our evening worship. It was dark except for the candles that lit the aisle. We each lit a small candle and placed it on a flight of steps at the end of the aisle as we left the service. During the service, Christine sang 'Come Holy Spirit Come'. The song wafted down from the balcony above the original arches of the abbey, and seemed to be ethereal, as if from angels in Heaven. A presence and a sure spiritual belonging – eternally beautiful, unfading, everlasting.

> Iona's Saints, forgetting not past days,
> Garlands shall wear of amaranthine bloom,
> While Heaven's vast sea of voices chants their praise.[6]

This service was a simple service of personal commitment to Jesus, and we were invited to return at 11 p.m. for half an hour of quiet reflective meditation.

I read on p.42 of the *Iona Community Worship Book*:

> By Thursday evening many in the abbey Church will be thinking about the situations to which they will return. The act of commitment can be a way of confirming the new perspective or healings or convictions that we have received on Iona, and thus help to prepare the path for integrating the Iona experience with our day to day situations.

I returned to the candle-lit chapel for meditation. Outside was quite black but this had been a lovely, sunny day and still the gentle breeze of the day remained. I remembered the Introduction to the Prelude:

> Oh there is blessing in this gentle breeze,
> A visitant that while it fans my cheek,
> Doth seem half conscious of the joy it brings.
> From the green fields and from the azure sky,
> What ere its mission, the soft breeze can come
> To none more grateful than me escaped
> From the vast city, where I long had pined,
> A discontented sojourner; now free
> I breathe again! Trances of thought and mountains of
>   the mind come fast upon me.
>
> Whither shall I turn,

> By road or pathway, or through trackless field,
> Uphill or down, or shall some floating thing
> Upon the river point me out my course?[7]

In accompanied silence we meditated.

I had further to go tonight as I left the chapel – past the Celtic crosses, past the front door of the abbey, past the garden of peace, along the gravel path that reached the lambs nestling against their mother; and in the foreground the stone arch that led to the sea and beyond.

> From nature and the overflowing soul,
> I had received so much, that all my thoughts
> Were steeped in feeling I was only then
> Contented, when with bliss ineffable
> I felt the sentiment of being spread
> O'er all that moves and all that seemeth still;
> O'er all that, lost beyond the reach of thought,
> And human knowledge, to the human eye
> Invisible, yet liveth to the heart;
> O'er all that leaps and runs and shouts and sings,
> Or beats the gladsome air; o'er all that glides,
> Beneath the wave, yea, in the wave itself,
> And mighty depth of waters.[8]

So I said 'goodnight' to the mighty sea, and fell into a peaceful sleep.

What happened next I find very hard to recount, and certainly difficult to record in my journal, where it is written in words that seem totally inadequate and unnecessarily indelible. However, I wish to write down faithfully what occurred, because so far I have explained to certain people only parts – parts that they might understand and parts I was able to speak of – because I could not speak of what occurred.

This was Thursday – late in the night – and we had returned from the service, calling for the Holy Spirit. We had lit individual candles of prayer, and some of us had spent half an hour meditating. I was peacefully asleep when I was awoken by screams, agonising screams and a cry for help. I established what I was hearing was fact and sat up with my legs over the bed. I felt for something to put over my shoulders and found a cardigan. Perhaps the person in the next room was ill. I would go and see if I could help, but the screams were not of pain so much as anguish and torment. I hesitated to assess what I should do, when a command came to me: 'Watch and wait', As the screams continued, I moved to get off the bed, but again came the command, 'Watch and wait'. I now took heed of the voice of authority speaking to me, and a third time quite clearly came, 'Watch and wait'. I had a feeling of presence in my room – the room was almost dark, but I could just make out shapes and the presence and the voice came from the door. I waited expectantly – I knew something was going to happen, but I had no idea what. I knew I had to 'watch and wait'. I felt safe and calm and knew I was not in danger in any way, but I felt impending danger. This feeling grew in intensity and a dog barked a warning growl, a deep and knowing bark, three times. I had never heard a dog on Iona before and this was my sixth night here. My window was shut but the noise of the dog came quite definitely from the window. Then there was a deathly hush – not a sound, no dog, no screams, nothing. And still I sat up waiting as I had been commanded. My heart was pounding against my chest, but it was in earnest expectancy – I felt completely safe in my 'cell'.

Surely, and swiftly and with a determination of purpose that made me gasp, the angel of death passed over my room, from the corner behind my bed to the corner on the right of the doorway. There was no waver or movement in its wings, as with a bird of prey. The black straight wings were sure, stiff and directed in flight to my room. The angel of death had appeared from the hill behind the Garden of Peace, on a mission of purpose, but when it came to my room it veered off at the right of the doorway and flew over the field, the ruined archway and over the sea. There was a second when the angel of death looked at the door and realised; and then lifted, altered his angle of flight and flew off.

I was aware that my room was full from corner to corner, like an impregnable fortress, with this presence, which I know now to be the Holy Spirit. I sat for a while and thought how safe I had felt and how nothing, not even Satan, can touch you if the Holy Spirit is with you. I know the Holy Spirit can come and surround us in a tangible way, in which we can hear and see and experience, and was as real to me as we are told in the Bible on the day of Pentecost.

I got into bed and fell fast asleep – but my vision was yet to come. I do not like to recount this – it was in the form of a nightmare and I was thrust into what appeared to be a gathering or party. I was standing on my own surveying a scene of debauchery. It seemed every perversion of every kind – when someone got on my back. I turned round and his face was twisted, evil and smirking. Someone else then jumped on my back as I faced my first tormentor. I turned and this went on and on till great numbers of evil and perverted people tried to jump on my back. They then tried verbal persuasion – this was a party, it was good to do this, everyone did this. I managed to get away. In the next second a fast-track train hurtled out of nowhere, heading straight for me. I jumped, using all my wits, and managed to leap out of the way. This happened again – hurtling out of nowhere, from a direction I knew not, straight for me. It was terrifying, but in a second they were gone and I felt tremendous relief. Then what appeared to be a digger – a huge piece of machinery – came towards my right side. It had flashing steel blades – rotating and slicing everything in its path – and it came for my right side. Mercifully, I used my presence of mind and escaped harm, but it had been terrifying. I lost consciousness for what seemed like a split second. I came to with the most awful realisation. I looked down at my body and I was wearing a despicable garment of lewd, red satin, and lace. I was horrified as the realisation dawned on me, that in that split second – a twinkling of an eye – I had been 'got'. Every emotion of horror, hopelessness, despair, acute disappointment that I had allowed this to happen, came to me – a terrible realisation that I had sinned. I got up and looked at my tormentors. They grinned and smirked at me; but then, amazingly, I turned my back, shrugged my shoulders and walked off. I watched myself as I walked off – straight, calm, not a care in the world. My body seemed to be white with a translucent lightness. A complete aura of peace and light shone around and through me. He said, 'You shall not be overcome.' In the weeks ahead it was this feeling, that no matter what, I could look back at that moment of pure peace and recapture it, which kept me calm. If I could shrug my shoulders and walk from my torment, this is what was possible, and I must do.

I have tried to establish when I was awake and when I was not. I heard screams which awoke me and I reached for my cardigan and put my legs over the bed, but stopped – this is definite, and others heard the dog bark, which also puzzled them. I was awake whilst I obeyed the command to 'watch and wait'. I knew in my wakened state the room was full from corner to corner with a presence of complete reassurance, I knew without a doubt I was safe, as long as I stayed in the room. If I had left the room I shudder to think what would have happened. When I realised the danger was passed, and silence returned, I got properly into bed and stayed sitting up, but at this point God put me into a trance. He then forewarned me of what I was going to face. I was perfectly prepared therefore for what I had to face.

Friday morning I awoke and went for breakfast – reassuring solid bread, porridge and spreads! Mavis and I mopped and cleaned the stone steps and passage as usual. I don't recall in detail Friday morning, it seemed to move in a haze, as though everything was taking place at a distance. We sang a chorus in the chapel:

> Dance and sing, all the earth, gracious is the hand that tends you.
> Love and care everywhere,
> God on purpose sends you.

Had I been sent to Iona with a purpose? Had God, on purpose, sent me? I stayed behind in the chapel and looked at the Worship Book open in front of me.

> Deserts stretch and torrents roar in contrast and confusion.
> Tree tops shake and mountains soar, and nothing is illusion.

The last line stood out:

> Kiss of life and touch of death, suggest our imperfection.
> Crib and womb and cross and tomb,
> Cry out for resurrection.[9]

Some workmen came into the chapel, climbed high up in the leaded window and began hammering and repairing a damaged window, so I left and walked my little walk round the gravel path. I did not go into the Abbot's house where my room was but walked on and sat outside the small museum, overlooking the sea.

The sky was blue, the sea was blue and calm – exactly as it had been the night before – the Thursday night I had walked from the chapel along the gravel paths to my room, at midnight.

I pondered over my vision and what it might mean. Why did the angel of death come so determinedly, and set on a course for my room? For a long time I acknowledged real evil in the world – but not in such a manifest form. I thought of God's chosen people ready for flight, each in his own room, having obeyed God, to sacrifice, pray and eat only unleavened bread – to put a mark on their door as a sign. Did they wonder what was to happen – did they 'watch and wait'. And when the angel of death passed over, did it sense God in their rooms and veer off – did it fear the sign over the door?

I felt an amazing confidence that God's people must have felt – even the angel of death feared to enter. The presence of the Holy Spirit is an amazing reality I had never fully understood before. I feel the Holy Spirit can be 'watered down' in our faith today. We feel it is something involved in our attitude of kindliness and good deeds – a good feeling. But what I witnessed was power, taking over me, filling the room from corner to corner.

> When the Day of Pentecost came, all believers were gathered together in one place. Suddenly there was a noise from the sky which sounded like a strong wind blowing, and it filled the whole house where they were sitting. Then they saw what looked like tongues of fire, which spread out and touched each person.

Power, described as tongues of fire.

> When they heard this noise, a large crowd gathered.

> They were all excited, because each one of them heard the believers speaking in his language.
>
> Acts 2, Verse 6

> Amazed and confused, they kept asking each other, 'What does this mean?'
>
> Acts 2, Verse 12

I thought over my vision and asked, 'What does this mean?' One of our party raced towards me and said she had been looking for me and that we were all meeting to discuss the journey home. So I quickly got up and ran back with her to the meeting.

Ann Smith said, 'Are you all right? Where have you been – we have been waiting for you?'

I reassured her I was all right, but I did wonder if I looked in any way different – I certainly felt different.

Mavis said, 'A window – a leaded window was blown out of the main window in the abbey chapel last night. Strange,' she said, 'because it was quite calm as we left our service.'

A small group of us went for a walk down to the post office and to the few shops on the island. We wanted to buy some souvenirs and post cards. We walked leisurely, and talked of new-born lambs, highland cattle, white sand and lapping waves. We remembered the stars in the sky that always shone so clearly here in the unlit skies. There was absolutely no hurry to our mission, and we were almost disappointed when we arrived at the shop. I bought a large postcard of the abbey and Bishop's house, with green fields in the foreground leading to the rocky sea's edge, and with the rocky outcrop sheltering the abbey behind. It was a view of a pristine and well kept building, but inside the chapel were some ancient weathered stone arches dating from the 1300s.

I bought a postcard of St Martin's cross in the foreground, and peaceful stretches of green grass, leading to a cobbled path and eventually to the church graveyard that has John Smith's grave – simple and unpretentious – in amongst the other graves. We seem to know more about John Smith; and this grave seemed to say more, than we ever heard about him when he was a public figure.

Another postcard was of the South Aisle Chapel. This was a small chapel separate from the abbey, and although it was dark inside with stone walls leading up to timber rafters, the sun darted and glinted as it penetrated the leaded lights in the oval-framed windows. There were several chapels on the island and I decided I must find time to visit these, and as this was Friday – time was running short. I bought another card with three Celtic crosses on – Maclean's Cross, St John's Cross, and St Martin's Cross. They had woven patterns, symbolising our life on earth woven into God's creation, and our spiritual life weaving directly into our earthly lives. With the circle solidly round the centre of the cross – all is one – I began to see God the Father, God the Son and God the Holy Spirit in a more definite and whole way while on Iona. It is difficult to find adequate words, except to say, as I prayed, I was aware of the Three in One, and the words Father, Son and Holy Spirit came involuntarily to my lips in a way I have never experienced before. I also bought a postcard of the abbey cloisters – looking a bit too newly rebuilt, but I could just see the two original columns that dated back to the thirteenth century. I purchased some souvenirs as reminders of Iona and then set off back for the abbey.

We were to have our last meditation, and we met at 11.30 a.m. in a small room off the cloisters. We separated into groups of four or five and were given a candle, and we were each given a sweet wrapped in gold, and a plain outer wrapper. The candle was lit and we were asked to place the sweet in proximity to the candle, in relation to our nearness (or distance) to God, the source of all light. We could do exactly what we wished with the wrappers and it was interesting to see the different responses to this task. I felt completely protected by the Holy Spirit and placed the gold wrapper so it touched the candle, and the sweet I placed on the transparent wrapper touching the gold paper. I remembered in my vision, how my body seemed to be white with a translucent lightness, and how a complete aura of peace and light shone around me: 'You shall not be overcome'.

Our last lunch of home-made soup – ladled out from a huge pot in the centre of the refectory – gave us the refreshment we needed to walk to all the chapels on the Island. We walked to the Roman Catholic chapel which had been built recently by Frances Shand Kidd – Diana's mother. It was a white, clean-looking building and was called a House of Prayer. As I walked in through the door I was followed closely by another visitor – she said she was a nun from Cornwall and was having a week's rest and holiday. The chapel was empty, and there were neat rows of chairs facing an altar, and behind the altar was a window looking out over green fields leading down to the sea. A notice said this was a prayer house for all denominations but that, when Communion took place, only Roman Catholics could take part. This seemed sad and I wondered how far we had come in unity since I had glanced back at my Jewish friend and my Catholic friend all those years ago. I gazed in wonder at God's creation in the window behind the altar. It was easy to feel close to God here, and easy to pray and thank God. I prayed for the nun who knelt silently on my right, and I knew she was praying for me.

From the newest chapel, we went to the oldest chapel – St Oran's chapel. This is the oldest building on Iona and it was restored in the eleventh century at the request of St Margaret, Queen of Scots. Oran is remembered as the first Columban Monk to die and be buried on Iona. So many chapels and places of prayer here amongst the beauty of

God's creation. The nunnery too, open to the blue sky, reminded me of, 'Not to the earth confined, ascend to Heaven'.

William Wordsworth wrote:

> Kind nature keeps a heavenly door, wide open for the scattered poor.
> Where flower breathed incense to the skies.
> Is wafted in mute harmonies
> And ground fresh – cloven by the plough
> Is fragrant with a humbler vow;
> Where birds and brooks from leafy dells
> Chime forth unwearied canticles
> And vapours magnify and spread
> The glory of the sun's bright head
> Still constant in her worship, still
> Conforming to the eternal will,
> Whether men sow or reap the fields
> Divine monition Nature yields,
> That not by bread alone we live
> Or what a hand of flesh alone can give
> That every day should leave some part
> Free for a Sabbath of the heart
> So shall the seventh be truly blessed
> From morn to eve, with hallowed rest[10]

Four o'clock and time for a 'wee sing' in the cloisters – sang 'Bound for that land', and then time to set the tables, and finally, our evening meal. The server sat at the head of the table, and the 'clearer-upper' sat at the opposite end, as usual, for the last time! Ron told us one last story about the 'Clown and Pope Gregory'. It was time to reflect on our week in Iona, and we met off the cloisters at 7.30 p.m. for reflections.

All the responses were positive – everything had gone

well from arrival and welcome, to the good, nourishing food, the varied services in the chapel and the enthusiasm of the young people leading us.

To bring our reflections to a close we were asked to sit in a circle, and were given a ball of bright, red wool. The idea was that someone would throw the ball of red wool to anyone in the circle. This person, having caught the ball of wool, would give one word to describe how they felt about the week. Keeping hold of the end of the wool, the ball would then be thrown to someone else, and they would think of one word, keep hold of the woollen strand and throw the ball to someone else. This started off very well – the first person caught the ball, pronounced 'peace,' and keeping hold of a strand of red wool, threw the ball to someone else. They in turn caught the ball, said 'prayer,' and keeping hold of a connecting strand, threw the ball again. The red woollen ball flew across the circle to the person on the other side. Unfortunately the wool slipped through their fingers and rolled under the chair. A helpful person sprang into action to retrieve the ball, only to get it fastened round the chair leg; so a second person came to help retrieve the ball, only to drop it round a central heating pipe. The ball by now – still with a strand attached and held aloft by the two who had successfully caught it – was out of sight. 'I can see it,' pronounced a third person, and lying stretched out on her front, she attempted to poke it from under the pipe. This was a cue for several others to attempt to rescue the red ball and rescue the game as well, which was by now in chaos. Half of us were on our knees unravelling the ball from around the chair legs, the pipe and anything else it was tangled up in; and the other half of us were helpless with laughter.

'Stop,' shouted our leader. And then she proceeded to pass the ball of wool quietly and sanely from one to the other in turn round the ring. We said our word and kept hold of the strand of wool. Eventually we were all holding up a piece of connected red wool in a perfect circle. Obviously God knew what he was doing and our chaos soon became whole and perfect, and as perfect as the circle on the Celtic cross. We were then passed scissors and cut off enough wool to wrap round our wrists, a reminder of our week, our friendship and our laughter – together.

We met in the chapel at 9 p.m. for our Friday evening service.

> Protect me, God, because I come to you for safety
> I say, 'You are my God; all the wonderful things I have
>   come from you.'
> How wonderful are your faithful people!
> My greatest pleasure is to be with them.
> You are all I need, my life is in your hands
> I am always aware of your presence
> You are near and nothing can shake me
> You will show me the path that leads to life
> Your presence fills me with joy,
> And your help brings pleasure for ever
> Amen

From Psalm 16

I looked up to the gallery above the oldest stone arches and remembered how the music and words, 'Come Holy Spirit Come', had floated down as if from heaven itself. I looked at the Communion Table of white Iona marble and with streaks of green serpentine stone that reminds us of this earth's evolution over hundreds of millions of years, and man's place on the earth, with a responsibility to care for it. Above the altar I could see the new pane of leaded glass, lighter and brighter than the rest. The abbey chapel was lit with flickering candles from the altar to the door. Outside the sky was lit with a million stars – hundreds of millions –

like the years captured in the marble altar, out of reach and unfathomable.

> Those who are wise will shine like the brightness of the heavens, and those who lead many to righteousness, like the stars for ever and ever.
>
> Daniel Chapter 12, Verse 3

The stars in Iona shine out clearly in the unlit sky and stretch for ever across the treeless island, unhindered, and down to the sea. I remembered Daniel's words, 'My Lord, what will the outcome of all this be?' In Iona under the stars it comes naturally to question the 'unfathomable'.

Saturday morning arrived and I got up especially early – the sea was still deep blue and calm, reflecting the blue of the sky above. I walked round the cloisters one last time before anyone else was roused, and sat between the two oldest pillars where the sun was managing to send a thin beam of sharp, bright sunlight between the roof and pinnacles of the abbey. I could feel the presence of the Saints, and the presence of many pilgrims who had come to Iona in search of healing. There was an infirmary for the sick where the museum now stands, and all were welcomed, lepers and many others. Sickness was often attributed to the devil, and the Saints, as well as using herbs, cured by exorcising or banishing malignant souls. St Martin whose cross stands outside the abbey, was a French Saint in the fourth century, who was able to cure the sick. The history of Christian Sainthood is one of pilgrimage by the suffering Christ, and he invited us to 'take up our cross and follow him'. To be a pilgrim, as we discovered on our wet and stormy Wednesday Pilgrimage, is one of suffering, as faith calls for sacrifice. Christ told his Apostles that the path they had chosen would not be easy in this world. So I thought of 'presence' and 'pilgrimage' – the two words that emerged with prominence during our talk on Celtic Spirituality. I thought of the powerful presence of the Holy Spirit, which I had felt and experienced in a way that I had never experienced before. This Holy Spirit had surrounded me, filled the room and protected me from death itself. Like Daniel, 'I heard, but did not understand.' (Daniel 12 Verse 8)

I felt I wanted to ask questions and I remembered how Daniel had asked, 'How long will it be before these astonishing things are fulfilled?'

God replied, 'Go your way Daniel, because the words are closed up and sealed till the end of time. Many will be purified and made spotless and refined, but the wicked will continue to be wicked. None of the wicked will understand but those who are wise will understand.' (Daniel 12Verse 10)

I began to understand suffering, sickness and sin. 'Your sins are forgiven, get up and walk.'

Everyone was beginning to gather for breakfast and all our luggage had to be placed at the abbey door, for the cart to take down to the ferry, so I hurried off to put my luggage with the rest of the cases.

We had our last porridge – served from a huge pan in the middle of the room – sensible chunks of nourishing brown bread and delicious spreads, and then headed for the chapel!

> O, God, our creator
> your kindness has brought us a new day
> Help us to leave yesterday
> and not to covet tomorrow
> But to accept the uniqueness of today.[11]

One last look at the ruined arch, the lambs eating peacefully beside their mothers, and the deep calm of the blue sea beyond.

> Deep peace of the running wave to you

> Deep peace of the flowing air to you
> Deep peace of the quiet earth to you
> Deep peace of the shining stars to you
> Deep peace of the Son of Peace to you.[12]

Along with the 'presence' and 'pilgrimage' of Iona and Celtic Spirituality, another word emerged with prominence – another word beginning with P – Poetry.

> Poetry is the breath and finer spirit of all knowledge
> Poetry is the first and last of all knowledge – it is as immortal as the heart of man
> Poetry is the spontaneous overflow of powerful feelings;
> It is emotion recollected in tranquillity.
> Poetry is the image of man and nature.[13]

So said William Wordsworth.

Chapter Three
Journey Back

The journey back on the ferries, the bus round Mull, and finally the coach all went perfectly, under blue skies, and with calm seas. We were soon on the coach and on the last leg of our long journey. As we helped ourselves to refreshment available in the middle of the coach, we had an opportunity to stretch our legs and chat to each other. My companion and I found we were discussing our faith and, in particular, suffering. We both found it difficult why we had to suffer so.

A verse from Philippians came to mind: 'For it has been granted to you on behalf of Christ, not only to believe in him, but also to suffer for him.' (Philippians Chapter 1, Verse 29)

Because the journey had gone well, we arrived an hour early in the church car park, where I was to be picked up by Bob. Gradually everybody disappeared as their chauffeurs appeared. Ann Smith said she would ring Bob and let him know I was an hour early and waiting for him, when she got home. However, she and Derek returned to the car park and said, as they had no reply from their phone call, they would run me home. I arrived home, thanked Ann, and then realised to my horror that no one was in and I had not got a key. So I went next door and rang Robert, my eldest son, who only lives half a mile away, and would have a key. To my surprise, Jamie my younger son answered the phone and said he was baby-sitting for little Samantha, and that Robert, Elise and Bob had gone out for a meal. He did not know where they had gone! I told him not to worry – there was nothing he could do, and so I rang my elder sister, who had a key. However, this being Saturday evening, there was no reply. I sat on my case in the drive for a few minutes, then decided to ring my other sister. Unfortunately she didn't have a key, but said, you must be dying for a cup of tea! So she came to collect me and we went to help Jamie baby-sit. What seemed like hours later, Bob and the rest of the family arrived, looking sheepish – but I had too much to tell them to worry about the 'welcome home'. After a cup of tea I was quite refreshed and talked non-stop. So life soon returned to normal. My pilgrimage to Iona, like my pilgrimage to Israel was an amazing experience and took on a dreamlike quality as I battled with everyday mundaneness. No wringing mop and metal bucket now, but sophisticated machines to set in motion. No gravel paths to wander along but the busiest road ever to drive along – the A6. What should be a fifteen minute journey, often took an hour at eight o'clock in the morning as I travelled to work, and again the same at five o' clock every evening.

The papers and television were full of the politics of a new government, and I realised not once on Iona had I read a paper, watched television or had one thought other than the spiritual life to be found on Iona. No time for a morning service, after a hearty breakfast of porridge, sensible bread and spreads – no time for breakfast! Certainly no mornings spent in meditation, and no dark evenings when only the stars lit up the sky. And so I rushed through the week on my return from Iona. Another week rushed by in the usual blur of work, looking after a husband and teenager, cooking, housework and so on. Several nights a week I was busy with activities connected with the church; Saturday, shopping and more jobs about the house and garden; and Sunday, helping with worship and resting. Next Saturday I was looking forward to a 'Quiet Day' at St Mary's, Alderley – this church dates back to the fourteenth century and I was looking forward to a peaceful day surrounded by lush Cheshire countryside. It was while making arrangements for this day that I discovered the bad news, that Margaret had been taken into hospital for a major operation. Margaret and I were real pilgrims together and had studied at Chester College together, become Parish Assistants, and worked in our various churches and eventually became Licenced Readers in the church. I was upset to see she was in such pain, but was comforted to know she was recovering well and going away to convalesce. It was years since I had been in the huge hospital, and wings and wards had been added – the local infirmary had been incorporated here with its emergency and accident wards. It was certainly a maze of corridors and people going here, there and everywhere.

Margaret told me, 'They don't keep you in here long – they have too many people waiting for the beds.' And so she was due out the following day.

I went home to pray for healing, and opened the *Iona Community Worship Book*. 'Each one of us is less than whole, yet because we belong to the body of Christ, we can also be instruments of healing, wounded healers for one another.' I read through the 'Service of Prayer for Healing', the Healing Service I had been destined not to attend during my week on Iona. This was a cue for a session of nostalgia and I laid the postcards out in front of me – the ones I had bought at the tiny shop. I spread my collection of wave–worn pebbles out, admired the marbled effect and the veins of green running through, and felt the silky smooth roundness in my hands. Before me was the blue sky of Iona – deep, deep blue and the sea blue and calm. The sun glinted on the leaded window panes of the abbey and recaptured the presence and spiritual belonging. My mind turned to the meditations, and how we had looked at the stepping stones in our lives, and what steps along our pilgrimage of life had brought us to Iona. We had searched our past for the five people who had an influence on our spiritual pilgrimage and some of us were surprised who came to mind. I was surprised when I realised William Wordsworth, born in 1770 and never knowing me or the world we live in today, had been a spiritual influence. I thought of the other four, and smiled at the memory of my maternal grandmother. She was small with kindly blue grey eyes and white curls about a neat face. Her eyes were clear and kindly and could sparkle, and yet they held the sadness of that generation, who knew they would lose at least one child, and accepted it. Indeed she lost her first born – twins at a few months old, and six children followed in quick succession, my mother the youngest. Her fourth child – a daughter with blue eyes and fine gold hair that framed her angelic and happy face – died of meningitis at the age of ten years. The remaining five children were left fatherless when my mother was two years old.

> A simple Child
> That lightly draws its breath;
> And feels its life in every limb,
> What should it know of death?
>
> She had a rustic, woodland air,
> And she was wildly clad:
> Her eyes were fair, and very fair
> – Her beauty made me glad!
>
> Sisters and brothers, little maid
> How many may you be?
>
> Seven are We

Two of us in the church-yard lie,
My sister and my brother;
And, in the church-yard cottage, I
Dwell near them with my mother.

Seven boys and girls, are we;
Two of us in the church-yard lie,
Beneath the church-yard tree.
You run about, my little maid,
Your limbs they are alive;
If two are in the church-yard laid,
Then ye are only Five...

The first that died was sister Jane
... So in the church-yard was laid;
And, when the grass was dry,
Together round her grave we played,
My brother John and I.

And when the ground was white with snow
And I could run and slide,
My brother John was forced to go,
And he lies by her side.

'How many are you then;' said I,
If two they are in heaven?
Quick was the little maids reply,
'O Master! we are seven.'

But they are dead those two are dead
Their spirits are in Heaven!
I was throwing words away, for still
The little maid would have her will,
And said, 'Nay – we are Seven!'[14]

My grandmother lived in the country with my aunt, my mother's sister. My aunt was born just a year before my mother; and my grandmother visited us for the summer months. This was part of our lives and I cannot remember a time when she did not come for the summer. Also I cannot remember a time when she could walk without the aid of a stick, and eventually a willing arm from one of us children. Today she would have a hip transplant and lead an active life, but just after the war arthritis of the hip was not treatable. My grandmother also came from an age when children were 'little adults', and were expected to help with tasks that would be considered dangerous today – and from an early age. She had her own room with a coal fire and I knew how to shovel coal on without getting too close or touching the hot surround – from the age of five years. If, when I heaped the coal on, there was a mass of black and just a weak flicker, I would get a sheet of newspaper, put the shovel upright in the grate, the handle just lodging on the tiled surround, and place the newspaper over the shovel. As soon as the flames leapt up and engulfed the grate in a mass of bright orange, I would snatch the paper away, scorched, before it burnt! One task my grandmother was very fussy about, was the ironing of her large white hankies with a blue embroidered initial in the corner – a fancy scroll of an initial. The ironing board was huge and heavy – the iron likewise – but the hankies had to be ironed perfectly on both sides, and then folded lengthwise three times and sideways three times, into a neat square. I would place the warm square on my grandmother's lap, with a feeling of satisfaction.

She would hold two corners and let the hanky drop, inspect it, and then I would know whether I had to unfold the iron from its asbestos stand, re-plug it and re-iron the not-perfect hanky. Fortunately this was not often and normally she would carefully refold the hanky and praise me, with an old fashioned saying – usually about a jewel in my crown! This broke my memory as I felt the smoothness of the jewels in my lap – the wave-worn pebbles from Iona. My grandmother was one of the five people who I had written down during our meditation with Martin, the vicar, as being someone important on my spiritual journey. She would arrive each summer with all the promise of sunny, happy, endless days. Sometimes my cousins from the country would accompany her and sometimes my aunt would come. We would chat happily and remember how my sister and I, only toddlers, went to stay with my aunt in the country during the worst of the war, when the bombing over Manchester reached its height. The airport where we lived was a particular target, and one bomb missed our house but left a huge gaping crack in the kitchen wall. My aunt always brought a huge box of chocolates, and we were sorry when she had to go! So why was my grandmother so important to my spiritual journey? Well, she had time, she could not walk unaided, so spent hours in her little oak chair with wooden arms and a burgundy seat. From there she ruled the house – or at least certainly us children. Apart from the hankies, there was the brandy! At least once a day she would say 'fetch me a drop of brandy – I don't feel too good today.' I was concerned how pale and tired she would look, and amazed at the rapid return to full spirits after a sip of brandy. There was the walking stick and repeated requests to fetch it and offer an arm as she went to the window, or return to her room. The endless letters that needed stamps and needed posting the minute the ink was dry. My grandmother came from a family of fourteen children, and they were all surely still alive; and then there were her good friends from Shropshire – so many of them who she could no longer see, and so they all received regular letters. When we became weary with fetching and carrying, our grandmother would quote a 'saying' and when we were really weary she would quote the one about 'Little Nan'. Now I can't remember how the lines went except it was full of good virtue and ended with, '... and little Nan does all she can.' And so I kept going! Well apart from the hankies, and the brandy, the stick and the endless tasks required, my grandmother, several times a day, would say, 'Fetch my Bible.' We had to be very careful not to leave any sticky marks on this or rumple any of the thin pages. The Bible was black and bound in the softest leather. The pages were tissue thin, and when shut, the golden edges to each page glowed in a wide band of encircling gold. The print was fine and neatly sloped in the italic form. We had other Bibles, but none as precious and impressive as this one. We felt it an honour to carry, and feel the soft leather. Sometimes we would creep away but often she would insist we pulled up a 'buffet' and sit quietly at her knees. She would read from the Gospels in the old English of 'thee' and 'thou' and long words of 'iniquities' and 'transgressions'. My favourite was 'Suffer little children to come unto me, for such is the Kingdom of Heaven'. Sometimes she would stop and interrupt the reading with a memory of the 'little angel' who died at ten years old from meningitis. Memories of how she could embroider beautiful flowers, crochet delicate mats and sew with neat stitches invisible to the eye. Then she would lean back and tell us to go because she was tired and needed a nap.

> Three years she grew in sun and shower
> Then Nature said,
> 'A lovelier flower
> On earth was never sown;
> This child I to myself will take
> She shall be mine, and I will make
> A lady of my own.'[15]

I had been back in the world for three weeks. It was the third Saturday after my return from Iona and I went to a

Meditation on the eve of Pentecost at St Mary's, Alderley. As I entered the church, I picked up a brief history and guide. It began, 'The approach to St Mary's from the main road is singularly beautiful. Following a lane flanked with cottages and under cover of great beech trees, the church buildings form a splendid group'. It mentioned the seventeenth century schoolhouse used until 1908. The nave and porch are late fourteenth century; as is the font, which was hidden in the churchyard for safe keeping during times of persecution and it was not rediscovered until 1821. There is an eighteenth century musicians' gallery and two unusual Bibles, one from 1717, called the Vinegar Bible, and another called the Breeches Bible. We sang, 'Spirit of the Living God Fall afresh on Me'. We looked at the signs of life in spring for it was May. The signs of life in the trees, still with fresh green buds but with the assurance that the fruits would come. We felt love, joy, peace, the fruits of the Spirit and the assurance that God was with us. There were nests in the eaves and we could see the watchful eyes of the mother bird protecting her young, which reminded us of the conflict between activity and freedom, our activity can so easily frighten this free spirit. We could see and smell the flowers of May – their scent all around – a seal of beauty and blessings:

> God put his stamp on you his stamp of ownership, by giving you the Holy Spirit he had promised. The Spirit is the guarantee that we shall receive what God has promised his people, and this assures us that God will give complete freedom to those who are his.
>
> Ephesians, Chapter 1 Verse 14

Outside there was the stream, flowing past Alderley Mill, past the churchyard, on for ever… streams of living water – signs of spring and of life:

> Whoever believes in me, as the Scripture has said, streams of living water will flow from within him. By this he meant the Spirit.
>
> John Chapter 7 Verse 38

Also, a gentle breeze stirred the spring trees – I felt I was experiencing a continuation of Iona; I could hear Christine singing 'Come Holy Spirit Come'. I looked up to the eighteenth century musicians' gallery, and remembered the old arches in the abbey at Iona and the singing as if from Angels in Heaven, and a presence and a sure spiritual belonging, eternally beautiful, unfolding, everlasting. I thought back to my 'vision' and remembered how the Holy Spirit had come to me, surrounded and protected me. This was the eve of Pentecost – just before the Holy Spirit came 'like a strong wind blowing'. Jesus said, 'It is not for you to know the time and season. But you will receive power that makes things work.'

I wondered what my 'vision' meant, what God was telling me. Had God sent me on a journey to Iona, had God on purpose sent me? I wandered out of the church with these thoughts, and found myself in the churchyard. I sat on a grave and was enclosed by a low wall going round the graveyard. I was surrounded by graves and began to read the inscriptions, and wonder about the people and their lives. What sort of people were they who died so long ago?

> Beneath those rugged elms, that yew tree's shade.
> Where heaves the turf in many a mouldering heap,
> Each in his narrow cell for ever laid,
> The rude Forefathers of the hamlet sleep.[16]

Gray in his Elegy goes on to describe some of the people with different personalities and different stations in life.

> The boast of heraldry, the pomp of power,
> And all that beauty, all that wealth e'er gave,
> Awaits alike th' inevitable hour,
> The paths of glory lead but to the grave

And in contrast he writes:

> Full many a gem of purest ray serene,
> The dark unfathom'd caves of ocean bear;
> Full many a flower is born to blush unseen
> And waste its sweetness on the desert air.

What sort of people were they who surrounded me? What personalities did they have. I wondered if they had the same feelings and thoughts as I have, or are the years too big a gulf, and would we have nothing in common? I sat immersed in these thoughts for a while and then moved to the low stone wall. I found myself overlooking a field and a gate, and through the gate the field dipped down to the river and a woody area beyond, opening up my vision, opening my thinking about God's love – away from myself; away from the people lying in the churchyard. This beautiful day in May spread out before me – the sun, trees, birds, buzzing creatures, wild flowers, the breeze – everything in God's world, so perfect. Even those people lying there; me, too – we have God in us, he created us, we can see, feel and talk to God – we can become more like God. He gave us his Son Jesus Christ; we can become, through him, the perfection we can see. We can grow more like God, we can become full of God, with his strength, peace and beauty and perfection, and leave our sin behind through Christ's death.

When I turned back to look at the graves, I sensed they were empty, the people and personalities were no longer there, or alive to me. God was alive to me and the joy of the risen Lord, who had freed us; led us out of the walls through the gate and beyond. Beyond to the horizon – to eternal life – on a journey, a journey that provides answers. I remember a friend asking me why we were not all like Mother Teresa, and implying we were no good as Christians. I knew this was wrong, thinking, but could not explain why, or how to put it into words, without being critical of what she was saying. Now I know why it was not a true statement – I can explain why, as with other situations that we know in our hearts, to be wrong, but cannot put into God's words. On that journey we can do this. As God explains, and things become clear, we know how to put over God's will, and we understand better his will, his being, and how he wants us to go on our pilgrimage.

From my seat on the low stone wall it seemed much clearer to me, I thought 'that was it' but I stood up and looked over the wall and saw on the other side some steps leading down from the wall. I went down the steps, followed the path – the path went on twisting and turning, 'it is never the end'. We never know why – there was more – a stream sparkled into view. Jesus said, 'It is not for you to know the time and season.' So I journeyed on along the path that twisted and turned – 'God is endless.'

Chapter Four
The Vision Unfolds

oday is Whit Sunday, or Pentecost, the fiftieth day after the Sabbath of Passover. It is the day the Holy Spirit came. It is twenty-four days since the Holy Spirit came to me in Iona and filled my cell, so nothing – not even the angel of death – could harm me. I was preaching at the early service in church and wanted everyone to feel this is an exciting day, a powerful day. Many of us could remember the Walks of Witness when the children would put on a special, best dress and a new pair of sandals, and carry flowers. It was a day to remember all year – in fact a day to remember throughout one's life. When the Holy Spirit came to the Disciples, it came in tongues of fire and the Disciples could speak in every tongue, so everyone heard in their own language (because there were many different peoples in Jerusalem). The bystanders were amazed and said the Disciples must be drunk on wine.

When the Holy Spirit came to me in Iona, it would have been simple to say the same thing, or that I was under the influence of drugs, hallucinating or dreaming. My feet were firmly on the ground and I reached for my cardigan, and I heard the dog bark outside my window.

The Disciples had previously asked Jesus questions. 'Lord, are you going to restore the Kingdom to Israel at this time?'

Jesus replied, 'It is not for you to know the times and

dates, but you will receive power when the Spirit comes.' With strength and power, comes reassurance, assurance and peace from God. We know the Holy Spirit is real and not wine induced, because we are given gifts to use and serve God with, and we see with our eyes the fruits, of love, joy, peace, and patience to endure all things.

I had questions I wanted to ask, but could only wait, but wait with assurance that the Holy Spirit would provide me with all I needed and protect me from harm.

We had been rearranging office furniture at work – moving heavy files, and generally having a good spring clean, ready to cope with new systems, and to streamline the office. The workforce like most places was cutting down on staff, and yet the work seemed to be increasing, with ever more duties falling on the few remaining. We were nearing the end of May and the weather was unique and beautiful to this lovely month. It was Monday after Pentecost and I had a check up at the hospital for a lump-like bruise that had suddenly appeared at the top of my right breast. I had a range of comprehensive tests, but would not hear the results for a week. I felt sure I had strained a muscle whilst moving heavy files from the top drawers of cabinets and was unconcerned, and the week passed quickly in work and various activities. Monday following was the Bank Holiday and so many were away for the weekend or the week, making the most of the Spring Bank Holiday.

I was back to work on the Tuesday to cover a colleague who was off for the week. Sunday of this Bank Holiday weekend was Trinity Sunday and I was preaching at the 6.30 p.m. evening service. The word Trinity doesn't appear in the Bible and is difficult for us to understand, but this Trinity is what we affirm every Sunday in the Creed – a belief in one God, Father, Son and Holy Spirit – each God and yet each a distinct person. This was discussed in one of the Alpha Groups I led recently – How God can be God and yet three persons, and it is one of the benefits of group discussion, where we hear each other's views and difficulties, and with the Bible, learn from each other. As each one of us goes on our pilgrimage, through this mountainous terrain we call our world, we need to look at the Old Testament, and the New Testament and we need to look at ourselves and our lives.

Right at the beginning of the Old Testament, in Genesis, we are told, 'In the beginning God created the heavens and the earth, the earth was formless and empty, darkness was over the surface of the deep and the Spirit of God was hovering over the waters.' In Isaiah we are told of the Son – the Saviour coming to dwell amongst us. In Isaiah Chapter 63, God says, 'Surely they are my people, sons who will not be false to me,' and so he became their Saviour. Also in Isaiah, 'The Virgin will be with Child and will give birth to a Son and will call him Emanuel' – which means 'God with us'. Reading on in Isaiah we read, 'A child is born and he will be called Wonderful Counsellor, Mighty God, Everlasting Father, Prince of Peace.'

These are well known readings from the Old Testament – familiar at Christmas – in which we see the Father, the Son and the Holy Spirit – One God in Trinity. Back we go to Isaiah and in Chapter 6 it says, 'The Spirit of the Sovereign Lord is on me, because the Lord has anointed me, to preach the Good News to the poor, to bind up the broken hearted, to proclaim freedom' – this was the passage from the Old Testament Scroll that Jesus read in the synagogue – because Jesus was the Messiah fulfilling this prophesy. After Jesus had read from the Book of Isaiah, he said, 'Today this scripture is fulfilled in your hearing.' Luke in the New Testament tells us the people in the Synagogue were furious and drove Jesus out. Another great prophet in the Old Testament, Joel, wrote of conversations he had with God and writes, 'God said to him, I will pour out my Spirit on all people – your sons and your daughters will prophesy, your old men will dream dreams, your young men will see visions'. Young and old, male and female are included here as God pours out his Spirit on all people. I thought back to Iona and my vision, God has said we will have visions, perhaps we are trying to ignore these visions; bury our heads in everyday business and we are not listening – only in Iona, away from the world, perhaps we are still and listen?

In the New Testament we read that an Angel came to Mary and told her, 'The Holy Spirit will come upon you, the power of the most high will overshadow you – so the Holy One to be born will be called "The Son of God".' When Jesus was baptised, the Holy Spirit descended on him in bodily form, like a dove. A voice said, 'You are my Son whom I love, in whom I am well pleased.' Jesus spoke of the Father who sent him; of Himself who revealed the Father; and of the Holy Spirit by whom He and the Father work. In John Chapter 14, Jesus says, 'I am the way, the truth, and the life, no one comes to the Father except through me – If you really knew me you would know my Father as well. From now on you do know him, you have seen him. Anyone who has seen me has seen the Father. Don't you believe that I am in the Father and the Father is in me?' Here we have Jesus distinguishing and yet clearly identifying with God in three persons. Last Sunday we remembered Pentecost and how the Holy Spirit came in tongues of fire, rested on each disciple, and they became 'on fire' and could talk in different tongues so they were all understood by the various different people in Jerusalem.

So what about us today? The Trinity is quite clear in the Old Testament and in the New Testament, but can we see this Trinity – this God as Father, Son and Holy Spirit, for ourselves – know there is one God, and yet see and believe this Trinity, be able to say with assurety the Creed? It is easy to see God at this time of year – God as our creator. He made everything, his nature is all around in the beauty we see, the abundance of flowers, growing trees, nesting birds, sun, rain, rainbows – only our great God could create such beauty and harmony, the wonderful peace that we experience when walking through his hills – perhaps in the early morning – when we are aware of a great God who cares for us. Isaiah knew this when he asked, 'Who has measured the waters, marked off the Heavens, weighed the mountains and hills – have you not heard the Lord is the everlasting God? The creator of the ends of the earth.'

Isaiah describes God well, he also describes men too. We read, 'Its people are like grasshoppers, he brings Princes to naught and reduces rulers of this world to nothing.' When I came back into the world from Iona, this fact was illustrated in our country for all to see. Immediately after the election – the resounding victory for a Labour Government – we saw Cabinet Ministers, who had been secure for years and years of Conservative rule, leave their mansions that went with the top offices. The Chancellor of the Exchequer, leaving Dornywood. Instead of arriving at Downing Street in limousines, they left on foot with no excited crowds or photographers waiting for them. 'No sooner are they planted, no sooner are they sown, no sooner do they take root in the ground, than he blows them away like chaffe.' We all witnessed this whirlwind for ourselves, so can identify with what Isaiah is saying.

The truths revealed in the Bible are not just historical facts, just words, we can see them lived out in our lives. 'To whom will you compare me, or who is my equal says the Holy One.' If we look at Mark's Gospel he starts with the most important truth. John the Baptist's message is brief, straight to the truth, 'I baptise you with water but He will baptise you with the Holy Spirit', and we read how the dove descended at Jesus's Baptism and God spoke, 'This is my Son.' Jesus was then empowered to go out, healing and teaching and performing miracles. We know there is a Jesus who did all this, and suffered and rose again, because apart from what we read in the Bible, we can see the truth of Jesus lived out – every day. We see Christ's truth being lived out in simple ways – we can read in the Bible of the Good Samaritan, and we know the person who helped us in our need, smiled and comforted us, the person who is doing Christ's work on earth, following his command 'To love thy neighbour'.

We know Jesus suffered, and we are told in the Bible, 'The world knew him not'. We can look at the world today and see for ourselves – the world does not know him. As a Christian doing Christ's work – following Christ's example – you know the meaning of suffering. You are against the world, Jesus said, 'If anyone wants to follow me, take up your cross.' We know Christians fall short – it is a steep, narrow path, following Jesus, but it is because we know suffering, sin, that we see the world of war and want, that we know Jesus.

At Pentecost the Disciples began talking in different tongues so all could understand. We can speak in a way that is meaningful to people, a way they can understand – the way of love and compassion. We can all serve God, young and old, male and female and we know we have the Holy Spirit because as we do God's work he gives us the gifts and enabling power. We get an assurance that we belong to God and the Holy Spirit gives us strength and power to serve God. We know inside we are motivated by something other than the world, something other than the material. From this indwelling of the Holy Spirit we see the fruits of the Holy Spirit – love, peace, joy, kindness, self control, etc. So we can feel and see the Holy Spirit at work in our lives.

And so Pentecost – the day the Holy Spirit came; and Trinity Sunday – God in three persons – and the Bank Holiday weekend passed. Tuesday was busier than usual as I tried to cover various absent colleagues, and keep ahead of my own duties at the Probation Office. Late afternoon I was due at the hospital for results of my previous tests to determine the mystery lump. I sat with many other patients, either waiting for results or treatment, and at last my turn came. I was shown to a side room and a nurse breezed in and asked my name. When I told her she said, 'Oh! the doctor has your file.'

I was told to wait and soon the doctor came into the room with a large brown file. He asked me to sit down in a chair and, leaning against the examination bed, he said simply and directly, 'We are going to remove your right breast.' He paused and looked intently at me and continued, 'This will be done as soon as possible – within the next two weeks.' He looked at me trying to ascertain my reaction and then said, 'Have you any questions.'

I reasoned it must be serious if my whole breast was to be removed – otherwise they would just remove the lump – so I shook my head, as I did not want to hear anything else at that moment. The doctor asked me to remain in the cubicle, and he smiled at me as he left and I said, 'What a shame.'

He hesitated and left. A few minutes later a nurse came in and held my hand and said she was very sorry I had had this bad news and asked if I had anyone with me, and would I be all right to leave alone. She would be available for me to phone day or night, and would support me through the operation and after. She gave me her card with phone number, and I left to find where I had parked my car. I must have walked past it three times, but eventually found it and wondered how I was going to tell my family, most of whom did not know of my mystery lump, or hospital visit. My operation was to be on the 11th June and I was to go in the day before to be prepared. There was so much to do – sorting out various problems at work, practical things at home like washing everything in sight and filling the freezer to overflowing, so the family did not starve. The rest of the week disappeared in a rush of activity – the 'Alpha' group on Thursday, and a special Service for all the churches in Hazel Grove on Sunday. Many who attended this Service had been to Iona on the Pilgrimage, and Martin the Vicar, and many others who had been on holiday were all back, or on their way back, and I could let them know of my operation. The Covenant Service between all the churches in Hazel Grove gave us an opportunity to meet and reminisce about our pilgrimage to Iona. I listened while the group recounted the highlights of the pilgrimage. The Healing Service was so wonderful but I could not join in because I had not gone to the Healing Service. Why had I not gone, why had a voice instructed me to remain in the abbey and not go to the chapel that evening?

I remembered the Service on the Thursday evening – the Service of Commitment when we called for the Holy Spirit to come. I remembered clearly the words written in the *Iona Community Worship Book*. 'By Thursday evening many will be thinking about the situation to which they will soon return. The act of Commitment can be a way of confirming the new perspectives or healings or convictions that we have received on Iona, and thus help to prepare the path for integrating the Iona experience with our day to day situations.'
The situation to which I had returned seemed unreal. Had I received from Iona something that would integrate my experience with my situation? Had I been sent to Iona, and prepared, warned? The first week in June passed in a haze of unreal and frightening thoughts. I was to have a major operation for something which is a feared killer, as feared as any of the plagues in ancient times. I had had my tonsils out when I was seven years old but never ailed seriously since. I had been so healthy, but now I felt strangely weak. I was going to have such a vital, personal part of me removed – not an extremity, but it seemed to be so close to the real me – my

chest, my heart, my soul. I thought, I might die. It was now Tuesday, a week before my operation and I still had many things to do and sort out.

I had to prepare for my 'Home Group' which met on Thursday, and on Sunday evening I was preaching at the Holy Communion Service at 6.30 p.m. The week passed in a haze of activity – I sat down late on Saturday evening with my shorthand notebook and pen and wrote my sermon – based on the Gospel reading from St John's Gospel, Chapter 15 Verses 5–11.

Our Gospel reading is quite short – just a few verses from John's Gospel.

When we read a passage from the Bible, we come to it in a certain frame of mind, and as we read the words, God speaks to us, as we are. He speaks personally and uniquely to each one of us. This uniqueness is very much emphasised in the Bible.

God knows us. He knows our weaknesses and he knows our strengths. We are told, 'He knows every hair on our head'. He knows our gifts, even when we don't, and if we are open to God, if we place ourselves in his hands, he will use our gifts. He will show us what we can do so that we work for his glory, to bring about his perfect will on earth. So as we listened to God's word, speaking to us tonight, each one of us will hear something different, as God speaks to us as individuals – in different situations facing different problems, different joys. We might have some wonderful news and be bursting with joy or thankfulness and God will pick this up. It might be the opposite to this and we might come to God fearful, or anxious, looking to God to reassure us, calm us. The wonderful thing about God is that he knows what is in our hearts, and he will speak to us individually, through all the diversity of our characters, all the maze of feelings we have; masses of people come to God – numbers are irrelevant. It is not easy for us to understand how we can be so important, so vital and so loved that God cares enough to speak to us directly in our situation.

Jesus said, 'I am the Vine.' Now I know nothing about vines and wine – as most of you know, I prefer a nice cup of tea, in a china cup! But Jesus said, 'I am the Vine,' you are the branches. Now we know grapes grow on a vine, on the branches, so branches are good. It is good to be called a branch – we are able to bear good fruit. We also know the branches grow out of the vine – the main supporting stem. Obviously there can be no branches without a main stem – the vine. The branches can do nothing, they cannot grow or bear fruit without the vine. It is the same with us – we can do nothing without Jesus, we can't grow as intended, and we can't bear fruit as God intended us to do. 'If anyone does not remain in me, he is like a branch that is thrown away and withers, such branches are picked up, thrown into the fire and burned.' We can begin to see why we are important, loved and cared for – if we are the branches to Jesus's vine. As Jesus says, 'If a man remains in me and I in him, he will bear much fruit.' We are in Jesus, living in his strength like the branches drawing strength from the main stem. We don't always know when we bear fruit. I was asked to type for a student, in his thirties, at work. I actually only typed a couple of things for him, he was mainly gaining experience in contact with the public. But I remember a conversation I had with him, where he wondered if he would find employment once he had finished his degree, and work experience, and we went on to talk about his wife, who was finding it difficult to secure a teaching post. The reason I look back and remember this conversation is because, when he heard I was going into hospital, he sent a beautiful card with beautiful words, and he sent his love and said he was praying for me – as if we had a deep bond, and yet I hardly knew him.

'If a man remains in me and I in him, he will bear much fruit.' Jesus adds, 'Apart from me you can do nothing.' Jesus then says, 'If you remain in me, and my words remain in you, ask whatever you wish, and it will be given you.' This is very reassuring, because we know we are his branches. We would not be in church here to worship God and draw strength from Jesus, if we were not part of the vine. So we can come to God in prayer and ask; because we remain in Jesus, we ask in Jesus' name. And there are more reassuring words, 'As the Father has loved me, so I have loved you.' I said it is not easy to understand how we can be important, vital, and so loved by God, but here we have Jesus telling us, 'As the Father has loved me, so I have loved you. Now remain in my love'. To remain in this love we have things to do. We must obey Jesus' commands 'to love God', and 'to love our neighbour as ourselves' – not easy to do, but we are branches of this vine and our strength comes from the vine. And Jesus said, 'I am the Vine,' so our strength comes from Jesus. Not only strength, but with this love comes joy. 'I have told you this so that my joy may be in you and your joy may be complete. We also have to bear fruit – 'showing yourselves to be my disciples'.

So each one of us has probably focused on something different. Perhaps we are assured how loved we are, perhaps we are drawing strength from this vine to do something we find difficult – to love our neighbour. We might feel able to come to God in prayer and ask, 'What you wish.' We might feel that complete joy that Jesus gives us. I was talking over this Gospel reading of The Vine with a colleague and as we looked at it together she said, 'It is very much about "remaining".' The word 'remain' is mentioned seven times in this small passage from the Bible. So we might focus on 'remaining', clinging to this vine, the source of our being and everything we need.

To the Glory of God.
Amen.

Chapter Five
Healing

Sunday came and the Holy Communion Service was to be a 'Healing Service'. Anyone who wishes for healing – physical, emotional, spiritual – or to ask for healing for someone they know, remains at the Communion rail after Communion, or at the end of the service and one of the clergy will pray for healing in body, mind and spirit, in the name of our Lord Jesus Christ. We robed for the Healing Service. The celebrant was our assistant minister, Rob Green, and I prayed my sermon might be well received and be God's words. As I stepped into the pulpit, Martin was sitting immediately below and was my immediate focus and support. When I administered the chalice, Martin, the vicar, knelt at the rail – I felt extremely privileged, re-affirmed and uplifted. Rob and I prayed for healing at the end of the administration, for those who knelt at the rail. I returned to kneel at the alter for the completion of the Service. After Rob had given the Blessing he asked me to remain where I was, and the choir and Rob processed down the aisle. I continued to kneel at the alter and eventually the church was empty and quiet.

Today was Sunday and on Tuesday 10th June at 9 a.m. I would arrive at the hospital for preparation for my operation on Wednesday. As I knelt alone in the church with my hands and head resting on the altar, I felt a presence. At first it was as though someone was kneeling beside me. I looked and no one was visible. I felt this presence go round me, over me – I seemed enveloped and immediately I went back to Iona. I now know this presence was the Holy Spirit, the same one that entered my room, filled the room completely and stood guard over the door, as I waited, sitting upright on my bed in the Abbot's room where I slept in Iona. I remembered my vision clearly – how the angel of death had come directly for me but was forced to turn and go over the sea. I realised for the first time, I was not going to die, had not God told me what was to happen. I also realised for the first time why I had not gone to the Healing Service in the abbey on Iona – the highlight of the week for the others. God had a different, greater healing. Hadn't Jesus delayed in healing Lazarus – Mary had come to Jesus in tears asking why he had not come to heal Lazarus when he lay ill – but Jesus had a greater healing for Lazarus, and raised him from the dead. Rob returned from saying farewell to the congregation and placed his hands on me, and asked God for healing in body, mind, and spirit, in the name of Jesus Christ.

I knew without a doubt that God had sent me to Iona, had spoken to me, to forewarn and prepare me for what was to come, and had told me, 'I would receive the power that makes things work.' I now knew the power of the Holy Spirit in a very real way and whenever I needed this power I would receive it. This was an amazing realisation, as amazing as the end of my terrible nightmare – I turned my back on my ordeal, shrugged my shoulders and walked off straight, calm, not a care in the world.

Monday evening I found a small case and began to pack the few items I would need – a lovely pale green nightie with intricate embroidery on the front from my elder sister, another shell pink nightie with small pearl buttons on from a friend at work; a peach lacy sponge bag with everything inside from facecloth to toothbrush in a pale peach, from my younger sister. A fresh lavender perfume spray, cucumber body lotion, special honey soap and moisturiser, and two fluffy towels edged in satin from various friends – certainly I was lacking in nothing!

I looked for my wooden prayer cross that Norman had given me a few days earlier – a small, solid and beautifully polished cross that just fitted in the palm of my hand. It looked a strange off-balanced cross, but the shape fitted perfectly and securely in my hand with my fingers comfortably locked round the cross. I placed it carefully on the fluffy towels, and went to look for a small Bible. I found one – the old authorised version of 'thee' and 'thou' but it had lovely, colour, plate pictures inside and they were finished in a silky, shiny surface. The dust cover had long disappeared, but inside the first sheet was a beautiful old-fashioned copperplate greeting. It said, 'To my great niece in the year 1947 from Great Aunt – 91 years.'

1947 and I had had my tonsils out – the last time I had been in hospital for an operation and now it was 1997! I had been sent to my cousins in London to recover, and my elder sister came too. I remember a long, long, hot summer of butterflies and sweet peas. My uncle was my father's eldest brother and very strict, we certainly all behaved impeccably in his presence. My aunt was very homely and always busy cooking and washing and cleaning. My cousins were great fun – two boys just a few years older than my sister and I. We climbed trees, made dens, had piggy-back fights and when we were supposed to be asleep in adjoining rooms, the boys made plasticine bombs and threw them on the connecting bedroom wall with a thud!

We had our jobs to do, and one of my jobs was collecting and podding the peas for dinner. I loved doing this and ate quite a few, in fact more than a few, and would have to dash into the garden and collect more so that we had a full pan of peas. Peas are still my favourite vegetable, and nothing compares to peas, out of the garden, out of the pod! The day our holiday came to an end was sad, we had had such a lovely, free time in glorious sunny weather. My aunt called us to say goodbye to our great aunt, who had her own room and did not even join us for meals. I have absolutely no memory of her except for this goodbye. She called me to her side. As she sat in a huge oak chair, she handed me the small compact Bible. She opened it to the page on which she had written my name and I saw '91 years' written in beautiful writing. I looked at her and thought how lovely she looked with pure white curls, and blue-grey kindly eyes and thought, 'I will live to be 91 years.'

I placed the Bible carefully on the fluffy towels and was just about to shut the case when the phone rang. It was Martin – he wished me well for 'tomorrow' and then he quoted from Mother Julian of Norwich – a mystic who lived in the fourteenth century.

> He did not say 'You will not be tempted.'
> He did not say 'You will not be travailed.'
> He did not say 'You will not be afflicted.'
> He said, 'You will not be overcome.'

I thought about this and my mind flashed back to Thursday night in my cell, and the nightmare – the party where great numbers of evil people jumped on my back and used verbal persuasion; the high speed trains hurtling out of nowhere; the digger with flashing blades, slicing everything in its path. How I had walked away. A complete aura of peace and light shone around and through me. It was the key to my vision. No sooner had I put the phone down than it rang again and Ann, the organiser of our Iona trip, was on the line, 'Everyone is praying for you,' she said. 'Everyone in Canada is praying for you.' I remembered our Canadian friends who had shared the week of 'Community' at the abbey in Iona. I remembered Ron's stories – I had brought back several tapes of his stories to enjoy in a quiet moment. 'In fact,' she said, 'the whole world is praying for you.'

She had put my name on the Iona Prayer Circle. 'Iona is the centre of a prayer fellowship of men and women from all over the world, committed to praying for people whose names are on our monthly intercession list' (p.37 Iona Book). It seemed impossible but was quite true, and made me smile.

I arrived with my case at the hospital on the dot of 9 a.m. The receptionist took my name, and then said, 'There isn't a bed, you will have to go into the television room to wait and see if there is anyone going home today.'
Bob looked alarmed and asked her what would happen if no one was going home, to which she just replied, 'Your operation will be postponed until there is a bed.'

I persuaded Bob to leave me and go on to work, and told him not to worry but to ring the hospital later in the day. I took my case and sat in the television room. I switched on the television and an announcer said, 'Today the 10th of June is the anniversary of the death of St Columba.' He went on to say this year was the 1,400th anniversary of his death and pilgrims would be gathering in Rome to travel to England to celebrate this. They would go to Canterbury and up through England – stopping at Chester, gathering pilgrims as they went. They would eventually arrive in Iona for celebrations of St Columba of Iona 597–1997.

What an amazing coincidence! but perhaps not a coincidence to God. I was to realise that every time there appeared any doubts or drawbacks I would immediately be reassured, 'All manner of things will be well.' A quote from Mother Julian of Norwich. I was told there was a bed for me at 12.30 p.m. I was shown to a bed at the end of the ward and told to undress and get in! I had no sooner done this than a beautiful basket arrived in white, gold and blue – iris and cornflowers, beautifully arranged with gold and blue ribbons, and a note wishing me well – from my brother and his wife. The nurse arrived with lunch, and we laughed as I said, 'I did not deserve flowers before my operation.'

After lunch I was trundled about to various departments for tests. One test, I lay perfectly still for three quarters of an hour on my back, whilst they put a flat plate like an ironing board over my body – just a few inches from my body. It moved very slowly down the top of my body. The nurse then came back into the room to turn the plate to the side of my body and it gradually moved down the side of me. She disappeared and no one came into the room whilst I was having this test.

I had various other strange tests, where I had dye put into me, with instructions to drink plenty of water. I did not ask any questions, just preferring to follow instructions. When I was returned to my bed the nurse hung a metal notice on my bed with clear black lettering, 'NIL BY MOUTH'.

My operation was to be about 2.30 p.m. the following day, depending on who was to be operated on first. Three of us in the ward of ten had metal notices, 'NIL BY MOUTH'.

Wednesday the 11th of June – the weather had been lovely for weeks, with the sky a clear blue and the various blossoms, cherry, apple, lilac and laburnum appearing in profusion, and a gentle breeze. But today it was overcast and grey, and rain was forecast. I met my surgeon for the first time – he breezed up to my bed, introduced himself, and drew the curtains briskly round the bed – a nurse and three students crowded round the bed as well.

He took my hand and said all would be well. He then produced a marker, told me to undress and clearly and surely drew a line round my right breast, and was gone. One student looked back and smiled – the nurse drew back the curtain and they all hurried to catch up with the surgeon.

This might be unique for me – to have my breast removed, but it was all in a day's work for the surgeon and routine for the nurse. One in twelve would have this, or a similar operation. I settled down to sleep with nine other people moving, talking, switching lights on and off. The ward was L-shaped and there were ten other beds in the other part for males as this was a mixed ward – so there was plenty of coming and going and plenty of noise. I found I was in quite a favourable position – being at the end of the ward I had a radiator on which to hang wet towels etc. Also, I had a bowl and mirror, soap and paper towels. As the doctors walked down the ward they would wash their hands here, but till then it was my 'ensuite'. At this end of the ward was a door which led into the television room and sitting room. Not many patients used this as most were having major operations, however if I propped the door open and sat back against my pillows I had an excellent view of the nine o'clock news!

I awoke early to the clatter of pots and feet – the ward was a busy bustle. Breakfast was brought round on trolleys, but the notice above my bed said, 'NIL BY MOUTH' so no one came near my bed! I asked for a jug of water and took a few sips whilst everyone else seemed to be eating porridge or drinking tea. After breakfast the anaesthetist came round to the three beds. 'That's Lysander,' whispered the girl from the next bed. I soon realised she was reading, *The Man who Made Husband's Jealous*, by Jilly Cooper. 'Lysander' asked me how I was, looked at the charts at the bottom of the bed and pronounced I looked very relaxed and so would not need a 'pre-med'. I did not know what a pre-med was so asked if the other two NIL BY MOUTH's were having a pre-med. When he said yes, I replied, 'Can I have a pre-med?' So at lunchtime when it seemed everyone else was tucking into roast beef and Yorkshire pudding, 'Lysander' brought my pre-med. It was a tiny blue pill which I soon swallowed and

I lay back to wait for 2.30 p.m. About two o'clock the nurse brought a blue gown and told me to undress and put on the blue gown, I began to feel a bit distant, and was rolled off the bed on to a trolley. I arrived somewhere that seemed like a side room with all sorts of equipment – it looked a bit like a junk room, or attic I thought. Then I thought no more.

I lost the rest of the day and the evening; and the next thing I remembered was three faces peering round the curtain. Somehow I was back in bed and wired up to various things, and drips. I recognised Bob, my elder son Robert and my younger sister – so I had had the operation, I was just lying on my back. I could not feel anything – no pain – nothing. I waved with my left hand and they left. I awoke to the clatter of pots and feet and remembered where I was. A nurse whisked the curtains away, took away the drip and said you can sit up, and even go to the bathroom.

'Can I have a cup of tea?' I asked and glanced at the top of the bed. The notice, 'NIL BY MOUTH', had gone. So that was it, I had had the dreaded operation and was sitting up drinking a cup of tea. At breakfast time I had porridge and bread and butter and another cup of tea – all was well! The nurses were kindness itself, very observant and aware. They helped me sit up. As I struggled, feeling like a beetle on its back, they helped me stagger unsteadily to the bathroom, and showed me how to put various bits of equipment into two Marks & Spencer's green plastic bags. I found it very difficult combing my hair with my left hand, and when brushing my teeth my hand kept going in the wrong direction.

The surgeon came round the ward in the middle of the morning, briskly followed by a nurse and three students. It made me smile and remember Sir Lancelot from *Carry on Doctor*. Everyone looked and discussed, and then left. The following day was the same and the day after – I drank my tea, combed my hair and brushed my teeth with my left hand. The nurse helped me to the bathroom, washed and tended my dressing and I lay back on my carefully arranged pillows – but I had not looked down.

Thursday morning, the day after my operation I had woken to find a table over my bed and on it the most beautiful arrangement of plants and flowers in all shades of pink, from delicate blush to deep, vibrant pink. It remained on my bed-table for my whole stay in hospital, and was the first thing I saw every morning – it was from my neighbour. I also received a bundle of letters and cards, and was amazed at where they had come from – our Canadian friends, my daughter in America, family and friends from all over, and many from the church. Every morning a nurse would drop a bundle of envelopes on my bed. 'Is it your birthday, again?' she said. I pinned them on the board over the bed but soon ran out of space.

Thursday Martin came and said a prayer by my bed. I felt at peace. Also on Thursday a Roman Catholic Chaplain, Sister Sandra suddenly appeared at my bed. She sat beside me and I told her about my pilgrimage to Iona and how I had only been back home two weeks when I found I was to have a major operation. She was calm and spiritual and she understood completely. She told me quietly that God had called me to Iona for a purpose. She then prayed and as she prayed she mentioned the saints. I shut my eyes and felt totally at peace – I felt no pain. She left quietly but I felt a presence still sitting beside me – it enveloped me round my head, into my neck, down my arms and I knew it was the Holy Spirit. Later on Thursday a patient who was waiting for tests and a diagnosis, came and sat on my bed. She was old, and was worried and unsure what was going to happen. I reached for my Bible and it was still marked at St John's Gospel, Chapter 6. We came to Jesus' words, 'If you remain in me, and my words remain in you, ask whatever you wish and it will be given to you.' She went to pray and ask, and was comforted. Every night I put my Bible on the bed at the side of my pillow, and took Norman's cross in my left hand. Open on my locker was a card with a little lamb cradled in Jesus' hands, 'My sheep listen to my voice, I know them and they follow me, no one can snatch them out of my hand.' (John 10, Verse 27) And so I slept with nine other patients – talking, walking about, and switching lights on and off. I was sleepily aware of a male patient wandering in and out of the TV room and watching the television at all hours.

The clatter of cups and feet told me it was morning. I drank my tea, ate my porridge and all was well. I had another 'birthday' and another pile of cards arrived at my bedside. I now had so many flowers that I took some into the TV room. I had a constant stream of visitors – family, friends, neighbours, work colleagues – popping in and out at all hours. Friday – Rob Green our assistant minister came and sat by my bedside – he brought prayers and greetings from many in the church. Nurses constantly arrived at the bottom of my bed to fill in charts, take my temperature, give me yet another injection – my left arm did not have any space left that had not been attacked by a needle! I was asked several times a day, by a nurse pushing a trolley laden with pills and medicine, if I needed pain killers, but I had no pain. The doctors arrived, pulled the curtain round and asked me if I minded the entourage of students. The students observed as the doctor checked the stitches, the clips, the two drains, and asked me numerous questions. The surgeon followed later, and went through a routine of checks and questions while a nurse took notes – it all seemed completely routine and I was one of twelve who would undergo this operation. Friday came and went and I still had not looked down. Saturday arrived with the familiar sounds of footsteps and clatter of pots – I ate my porridge and bread and butter, drank my cup of tea and felt strong enough to resolve this would be the day I 'looked down'. I collected my toiletries –

the moisturiser, the perfume, the peach lacy bag and one of the peach fluffy towels and set off with resolve. I was feeling stronger and yet I struggled with everything. I struggled to turn the bath taps on. With my left hand everything seemed to be out of reach. I simply could not move my right arm sideways. I wondered if I had been wise, I felt exhausted and thought how much easier it would be to get back into bed and let the nurse wash and tend me.

Strength surged through me and I looked down – my eyes could see quite clearly but my brain could not understand the message. I was looking at a blank sheet of paper – I knew there were words but I could not see beyond the white blank sheet. I fell exhausted into bed and awoke to see visitors arriving – my brother was passing by from a visit to Scotland and called in on his way home down South.

Sunday, and yet another 'birthday'. Flowers galore, some from various churches in Stockport who ask the members to bring them to someone in hospital. I shared them round the ward – and we were in a garden! I gathered up strength and 'looked down', but still no words – just a blank sheet of white paper. I remember reading that the nerves in the eye send messages to the brain at two hundred miles an hour, but to me as I looked at what had happened I felt no connection, not even one mile per hour – it did not seem possible what had happened to my body. Sunday and I reached for my Bible, my cross and my card with Jesus' hands – I felt the now familiar presence – round my feet, legs, up my body and into my neck, round my head. I remembered my vision in Iona and began to understand – it began to make sense and I saw how my vision was taking shape.

Did not the angel of death come for me – come very close to within a few feet of my bed as I lay there? But was I not protected by the Holy Spirit who stood guard at the door and then filled the whole room making it into a fortress? And there I lay in hospital with the same protection and surely the angel of death had gone – over the sea. I had been close to death, tempted, travailed and afflicted – I remembered the digger with flailing blades coming for my right side – it had happened, but now I would get up, shrug my shoulders and walk away. I had lunch and yet more visitors, and felt well on the way to recovery.

I reached for my shorthand notebook and pen, and wrote:

Passing Through – 15.6.97

It's me, and I am passing through.
I've stumbled on the fields of green,
Clouds have gathered on my sky of blue,
The gathered bluebells from the wood
Wilted to my touch whilst I stood.
Yet, a great creation I have seen!

I followed paths where e'er they led,
Through tangled ferns and undergrowth.
My heart's landmark spread overhead,
I thought not, nor could understand,
A foreigner in his native land.

The owl haunts the darkest night
The sunbeam loves the darkest shade
And sets the brook alight.
The fallen tree stands reborn,
From stately oak to lowly thorn.
A great creation has been made!

Golden fields lived beneath the sun,
Yet wilted in my hand
And when the setting sun had gone
And flower had had her fill
The night, and I, and time stood still,
Free to pass, but made to stand.

Free to pass, but made to stand
Upon this captive earth,
Yet I am passing through –
An end in view, a humbler birth
Where sunbeams penetrate the densest shade
To light the great creation that was made.
It's me, and I am passing through
But who are you?

Chapter Six
You shall not be Overcome

And so Sunday passed and Monday came, nearly a week since I arrived to prepare for my operation. I was feeling stronger. Whenever I felt the slightest hint of weakness or pain or sadness, something would happen to reassure me. A visitor would arrive, more flowers, more cards or a letter would come immediately, so I had no time to dwell on my situation. Today was no exception – I returned from my excursion to the bathroom and the realisation that my eye could still not send a message to my brain that could be interpreted as normal, still the brain could only see a blank sheet of paper. There were words, but my brain could not see them. Perhaps tomorrow would be clearer?

When I arrived back at my bed, I had missed the surgeon's visit yet again. Every time he came to check on me, which varied enormously so I could not plan to be in place in my bed for him, I was somewhere else. He obviously presumed all was well if I had the energy to be gallivanting around the hospital complex, and I never saw him again! However, there was a large brown envelope waiting for me from America. It was from my daughter Melanie. She had 'surfed' the Internet and come up with some relevant and interesting poems. Several by Wordsworth of course, some by Keats. I read the first verse of 'To Hope' and felt uplifted.

> When by my solitary hearth I sit
> And hateful thoughts unwrap my soul in gloom;
> When no fair dreams before my 'mind's eye' flit,
> And the bare hearth of life presents no bloom;
> Sweet hope, ethereal balm upon me shed,
> And wave thy silver pinions o'er my head[17]

I thought about these 'hateful thoughts', and the bare hearth, and likened it to my thoughts; and Keats' bare hearth could be likened to my blank sheet of white paper – where I could see no comforting words, although I sensed them there. Perhaps Keats' 'ethereal balm' would become my angel and wave her silver wings over my head! I sighed and moved on to a poem by John Betjeman – it brought back memories of when my daughter Melanie was seven years old and we both met the Poet Laureate and had tea with him. I read through his poem, 'Cornish Cliffs', where he says:

> ... And in the shadowless, unclouded glare
> Deep blue above us fades to whiteness where
> A misty sealine meets the wash of air[18]

It summed up my feelings which seemed to be wrapped up in a mist. I thought back to Iona. 'It is a very thin place.' The founder of the Iona Community, George MacLeod, said this. Also he said, 'There is only a thin separation between spirit and matter.' To be a pilgrim in Iona one has to look for the spiritual at the heart of the physical world. I turned over the sheets of poems, lost in a haze of beautiful words. I came to a sheet which said, 'from the Riverside based on Works of Chaucer.' It was in old English and looked like a foreign language but it made me smile to see the quaint spelling and phrases. There was only one line, which was repeated at the end of each of the four verses, that I could understand, 'And troothe thee shal delivere, it is no drede.'

The day ended with thoughts of a bare hearth; blue fading to whiteness; misty sealine; a thin separation between spirit and matter; and still my eye could only see a blank sheet of white paper.

I settled down and remembered some lines of poetry I had composed a few years ago...

> Where is all I know, familiar, right?
> Why is it with my eye, my mind can't see?
> Today just dawned and quickly passed away
> For now it is the evening of a lovely day;
> And words float through my mind like in a dream
> Half real, half day, half night, half of what has been...
> ... The misty evening, like my memory,
> Confused, wonders which way to grow, or die,
> With eye and mind and heart, that cannot see.

Perhaps tomorrow I would see the mist lift. I put my poems away and gathered my armour around me – my Bible, my cross, and my card with a lamb nestling in Jesus' hands.

Tuesday and I had now been in this bed for a week and was quite used to the regime. I was filling in the menu for the following day's lunch and evening meal, when the doctor came breezing past followed by his retinue of nurses and students. He hardly stopped as he announced, 'You can go home today.' One of the students gave me a sympathetic smile as she rushed off to the next ward and round of consultations. I was left to sort out with the nurse when I could go, and how I was going to organise my journey home – with mountains of cards and flowers and unsteady legs!

I ate my last lunch and packed my belongings and moved

into the television room to wait for my lift home. There were two anxious and elderly ladies waiting for a bed. I told them not to worry – I had just left one bed, and another patient was hoping to leave later on in the day, after her doctor had seen her.

I looked through the window waiting for my lift home and the sun shone brightly on the laburnum and the maturing trees. I gathered my belongings, not forgetting the basket of deep pink flowers that had remained on the table over my bed, and was the first thing I saw every morning as I opened my eyes. As I passed reception I left a huge box of chocolates, thanked the nurses for their care and assured them they had seen me for the last time. The lunch trolley clattered past me laden with empty plates and cups and I smiled as I thought this time I was not awakening to the sound of clattering pots and feet, but departing. All was well!

If I had any doubts as to how I was going to cope once I returned home, they were soon dispelled. Family, neighbours and friends seemed to arrive at just the right moment, and I sat back and watched everything fall into place. I thanked God continually for the amazing coincidences that occurred daily – even hourly. If I felt hungry something would just appear – a friend passing with a ready-prepared salad lunch, and another arrived as I ate the last mouthful of salad, with a bowl of raspberries from the garden! If I needed company a welcome visitor would arrive with the latest news or gossip. A steady stream of cards and notes wishing me a speedy recovery arrived at the most opportune and needy second. Friends bought or lent me books, so I was never short of a good read and stimulation. One of the clergy or a visitor from church would appear, to revive my spirits, at exactly the right moment. It made me smile to think how carefully and perfectly my coincidences were planned, and I felt sure God smiled.

The first three days at home slipped by as I arranged yet

more flowers, and cards, or sat in the beautiful June sunshine which returned as soon as I arrived home. My days were filled mainly with visitors, reading, or attempting to exercise my arm, and do the physiotherapy I had been advised to do. It was now over six weeks since I had been on my pilgrimage to Iona – six weeks since my vision and looking back I now see what God had been telling me, preparing me for, and warning me about. Hadn't I been through the nightmare once in my vision, and now in reality. I thanked God for preparing me so perfectly in a vision that the reality also was so perfect. Hadn't I seen in the vision how I had stood up, shrugged my shoulders and walked away, and that is what I must do. Friday 20th June – almost the longest day – I was awakened to sunshine and birdsong and that day I was to be relieved of the clips and stitches that seemed to be holding my right side together.

I apprehensively sat back while the District nurse undressed my wound to remove the clips. I watched her intently and noted the look of horror that she could not conceal; and she struggled to remove the clips. Eventually she decided to phone the hospital and arrange for me to go and have the stitches and clips taken out in hospital. So only three days after telling the nurses they had seen the last of me, I was back with clips that would not come out. A senior nurse gave me two strong pain killers and then attempted to remove the clips which are like staples. Apparently they had disappeared into the skin so it was very difficult to remove them. They shot out all over the room, some hitting the ceiling and rolling under the bed where I lay. I began to laugh and soon the nurse, relieved the clips had finally been removed, began to laugh and on our hands and knees we searched for the stray clips from under the bed. I arrived home and promptly fell asleep but felt no pain.

Saturday 21st of June – the longest day – and I awoke early but the sun had been up hours and was mature and yellow on the field of buttercups visible from the bedroom. The garden had been neglected this year and yet was a riot of colour. Californian poppies in bright orange and yellow grew in abundance in every spare space. Blue cornflowers had run riot through the flower beds, and the roses unpruned and unchecked were blooming as only June roses can! The apple trees had been a mass of blossom when I returned from Iona, and now there were green bubbles with black coronets where the petals of blossom had been, waiting to swell in the sun and showers into juicy fruit. All this wild beauty reminded me of a poem I had written – it was a long poem about the May Queen and the beautiful month of May called 'The May Day Dance', but I drew a few lines from this long poem into a short tribute to summer's longest day:

> Summer wildly spreads her charms
> With rosebuds gathered in her arms.
> Points to the violet with averted eye,
> Attendant with the pale anemone
> And sweet primrose, pale beneath the sky.
> That all may decorate her wood,
> And proclaim her spirit nigh.
> The summer's come to all the dale
> Her valley, hill and field
> Where e'er she leaves her breath of life
> And trails her leafy veil.
> And all may drink of beauty's dew
> That decorates her hopeful hour,
> With image of the perfect day.
> A living proof within a dream
> Perfection offered in a flower.

The longest day had indeed been perfect and as I settled down at the end of this lovely day I gathered my armour around me – my Great Aunt's gift – my Bible, my cross and my card. I slept perfectly and as I opened my eyes the following morning I was aware of two people bending over my bed – two 'old ladies'. I looked and focused and they disappeared. I dismissed this as a dream, but the following morning when I awoke, immediately over my head were the two 'old ladies'. I had been sleeping on my back, propped up by several pillows for comfort and clearly saw two old ladies bending over me. I did not recognise them but saw they had round faces surrounded by white curls and their eyes were a bluey grey. I recognised them to be the two old ladies who I had seen the morning before, so it wasn't a dream, and as I said, 'Oh! It's the two old ladies,' they disappeared. I felt puzzled and wondered who they were and what it meant, but I felt at peace and pleased to see them and hoped I would see them again.

So it was with expectancy and pleasurable eagerness the following morning that I opened my eyes and again – the two old ladies were bending over me. As I looked intently trying to understand what I was seeing and who they were, the two old ladies looked at each other, smiled and said, 'She is all right now.' As they acknowledged this they disappeared and I lay on my pillows totally at ease and at peace – and I never saw them again.

Today was mid-summer's day, the sky was deepest blue and the sun at its height. The blossom and Spring was yesterday, and today everything shone in an aura of peace and light with promise of fruits to come. My daughter in America rang to say she would be arriving at Manchester airport on Saturday for a week's stay. Today also is the Feast of St John the Baptist – I was surrounded by reminiscences of Iona – in the blue sky and the breeze and the memory of Saints. My pilgrimage to Iona with all its amazing experiences, that had taken on a dreamlike quality on my return to the real world, was unfolding in reality step by step as surely as the stepping stones that had guided my feet. I had received my vision, I had seen it become reality, and out in this summer breeze I recognised the Holy Spirit – the same one that had come so unexpectedly to turn my cell into a fortress, so even the angel of death feared to pass by. I had felt the touch of death but now I was calm with not a care in the world. I felt upright, white with a translucent lightness – a complete aura of peace and light shone around and through me.

'You shall not be overcome.'

God had surely directed my stepping stones to reach Iona, and experience the saints whose presence I felt so closely. Were not the saints known to have the ultimate healing power – the ability to bring the dead back to life? The day after my vision on Iona I had dressed quickly and left my secure cell and sat sheltering against the museum wall which had been the refuge for the sick. Here, in St Columba's day in the sixth century, those suffering from leprosy and the plague and all manner of disease had sheltered. one thousand four hundred years later I was unknowingly seeking the same refuge.

> The history of Christian sainthood is a long path strewn with thorns and the suffering of individuals bearing the cross in the name of their belief. The apostles were warned by Christ himself that the choice they had made exposed them to death, and this would always be the case. To believe is, in Christian terms, to suffer, and faith calls for sacrifice. The history of sainthood in the Christian tradition bears witness to this fatal combination in countless ways.

This is a paragraph taken directly from *The Saints – the Chosen Family* by M. Dunn-Mascetti.

I had felt the kiss of life, and seen the Power that makes

things work.

> Protect me God, because I come to you for safety,
> You are my God, all the wonderful things I have come from you.
>
> Psalm 16

So my pilgrimage, my journey of faith so uncertainly embarked upon, was providing answers, was showing the well-trodden path ahead, and the Lord was already there.

Chapter Seven
Farewell to Summer

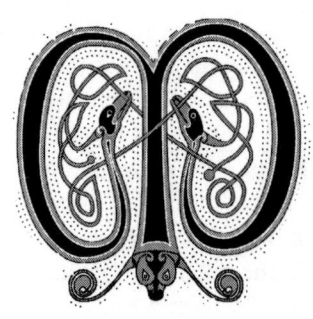

My daughter Melanie arrived after a thirteen hour flight from San Francisco, and we spent the weekend catching up on news from America, all thoughts of the usual jet lag completely forgotten. We had spent the Easter of 1996 in San Francisco at my daughter's apartment. Bob and I were amazed at the hugeness of everything – the coastline went on for ever. My youngest, Jamie, was impressed with the restaurants, eating places, bars, and the size of the meals. We laughed as we reminisced over one meal of ribs and spaghetti, where we never found the spaghetti under the pile of ribs, mushrooms and vegetables. We spent three amazing weeks visiting places that previously were simply words in songs like Monterey, San Jose and Las Vegas; or places on maps. Everything was larger than life here, the tallest building, the longest beach, the most famous bridge, the Golden Gate Bridge; the island that once housed the most dangerous prisoners, Alcatraz; and even the trees were the tallest and oldest in the world – the redwood trees. The climate – too, the most perfect blue sky, sun and heat, always cooled by a balmy breeze. The apartment did not have one balcony but three, and so we moved with the sun, taking our drinks and reading matter with us. There were always the tennis courts and swimming pools if we felt energetic, or simply a stroll in the apartment grounds with its lake, waterfalls and fountains was sheer pleasure. And so we happily recounted our blissful holiday in San Francisco, going on the cable cars, to shop at any hour of the day or night. At this point my daughter announced we were going shopping for a complete new outfit, and so I went shopping for the first time since my operation. The following day – Tuesday and two weeks since I left hospital and less than three weeks since my operation, I had to return to the hospital for a check up. The doctor seemed pleased with my progress and said I did not need to return for another check up until October. 'All manner of things will be well.' A quote from Mother Julian. We spent a lovely, sunny week together and on the Saturday before Melanie had to fly back to America on the Sunday, we joined in a reunion lunch at church with all the pilgrims (from the churches) who had gone to Iona. We each took a 'dish' which combined to provide a great feast and we remembered and shared our experiences of Iona, and swapped photos!

It was now July, and had all this happened since I took those faltering steps to Iona with my fellow pilgrims? It all seemed like a dream, it was a dream, it was a dream that had become a reality. I understood exactly the meaning of the dream, and was thankful beyond words that I had been so amazingly prepared and warned. I felt compelled to record faithfully every detail and emotion, because as I recovered from my operation my vision began to fade. I returned to normality so quickly and went about my daily routine as before. Every now and then my youngest Jamie would say, 'Have you done your exercises?' or 'You're walking lop-sided,' or some similar youthful comment intended to make me aware, that no matter how hard it was, I must make an effort and return to my former self. I was still off work, and was unable to drive but every other aspect of my life continued as before. I joined in a Working Party for a day with my work colleagues – it was to discuss and plan our working year ahead. My bridge parties began again in earnest as we drank coffee and ate chocolate biscuits. I resumed my duties at church – up in time for 8 a.m. Communion, thankful to be alert and well enough to read the lesson and preach and say the prayers. Every Friday my elder sister who left work at lunchtime, came for lunch and we would go out for the afternoon, walking, sight-seeing, or looking round a museum or stately home. It was the end of July now but the days were glorious, sunny and warm and the evenings balmy and light. We would treat ourselves to an afternoon tea or an early evening meal and so July passed into August

> All through the endless days of summer time
> We met beneath the merging bowers or would roam
> Among the hills of wild thorn and wild gorse
> And wherever we sank to rest a while
> We called our natural home
>
> As summer's timeless hours passed by
> We merged with every natural hue
> Part of the earth, part of the sky
>
> Extracts from a long poem Catherine Orchard

August turned out to be a real holiday month of happiness and heatwave. We spent a week in the Cotswolds with my brother Tony and his wife Jenny, and as they have a huge rambling house in five acres, we set off happily with a loaded car. My husband Bob at the wheel, myself, my youngest, Jamie, and my younger sister, Gillian and her daughter Helena plus various items of luggage and cool-box and picnic basket all piled into one car. We headed for a week of fun and freedom in the beautiful Cotswolds. We usually manage to visit for one week in the summer holidays and this year was to be no exception. The week passed by in laughter and barbecues, surrounded by dogs, cats and green wellies. The night before we were due to return home was always a wild celebration, and so we ate a wonderful evening dinner cooked to perfection because Tony is a trained chef and his wife Jenny a Cordon Bleu cook. We had wine and liqueurs and talked until midnight, and then decided on a midnight walk. Out in the deep countryside of the Cotswolds, the night is pitch black, the only light from the moon and stars. I decided to retire and so the others set off with only the moon, stars and a torch.

Something about the night reminded me of De Quincey, that strange poet who wrote the *Confessions of an English Opium Eater*. I was glad to let the others go and explore the night. I would prop myself comfortably up on pillows and drift into sleep. As I drifted into sleep words of De Quincey came to me – he was educated at Manchester Grammar School and was a young man in Wordworth's day. He plucked up the courage after several attempts and visited William Wordsworth (at Dove Cottage) in the Lakes. However I don't think it was a successful meeting as De Quincey was totally overawed by the wonder of this great poet.

De Quincey wrote:

> ... Whilst the dead hours of night were stealing along,
>   all around me...
> Wild it was, beyond all description,
> Black as...[19]

My mind drifted as I thought of De Quincey's words. I thought back to Iona and my vision and so much had materialised but I still did not know the outcome. I remembered the night before my operation and how I had thought, I might die.

De Quincey thought death was particularly hard to come to terms with in summer – everything growing, birds singing...

Ever since I was a child – my earliest recollection, in fact, was of a blackbird singing. I was born in the middle of the day, in the middle of August – in the middle of Sunday lunch according to my mother, and I feel sure I heard a blackbird singing.

De Quincey's words returned to my sleepy mind...

A golden day of sunshine slept
  Upon the woods and fields, so awful was the universal silence, so profound the death-like stillness.
  A day belonging to a brief and pathetic season of farewell. The last brief resurrection of summer in its most brilliant memorials, a resurrection that has no root in the past, nor steady hold in the future, like the lambent and fitful gleams from an expiring lamp, mimicking what is called the 'lightening before death'. Slips into the noiseless deeps of the infinite, so sweet, so ghostly in its soft golden smiles. Silent as a dream and quiet as the dying trance of a saint – farewell to... farewell to Summer.[20]

I fell asleep.

Chapter Eight
Two Angels

The heatwave continued throughout all of August, and one particular hot and sunny day in the middle of August we set off – my elder sister and I – to the little village in which we sought refuge during the war. My Aunt had long since retired to the seaside and although we sent cards, and caught up on a whole year's news at Christmas, we had not seen my Aunt for many years. This time it was my turn to give my Aunt a huge box of chocolates, and the warm welcome, hugs and kisses over, we got down to some serious catching up on life. Had so many years really gone by – where were they?

'I don't think I would have recognised you, if I hadn't known you were coming,' my Aunt began – and certainly I would not have recognised my Aunt or my cousin. My Aunt was now in her eighties; and had become quite frail and found it difficult to walk – she was dark haired and a bundle of life and energy when we last met her. As we talked, her conversation became animated and I caught glimpses of my Aunt as I knew her – small and lively and always with a ready smile and yet kindly and helpful. My Aunt was the only one left now of my mother's family – of the four sisters and one brother, who survived into adult life. She was next to the youngest, my mother being the youngest.

We had tea in beautiful fine china and then continued our happy chatter of days gone by. As we remembered our grandmother, and the hankies and the brandy, my Aunt disappeared into another room saying, 'Before you go I have something I want to give you.' She returned with a parcel wrapped in tissue paper and handed me the parcel. I carefully opened and unwrapped the tissue paper and there lay my grandmother's Bible. I could hardly believe my eyes, that this was the Bible we had only been allowed to touch when given permission by my grandmother to, 'bring my Bible.' My Aunt explained that inside were the instructions given by my grandmother to my Aunt in 1927, when the Bible had been bought. My Aunt was twelve years old and was given a note of instructions as to what sort of Bible she must buy. The note read:

> The Bible is to be the authorised version translated out of the original tongues. To be printed on fine India paper. The lettering to be in fine italic and the pages edged with gold leaf. The Bible to be bound in soft Moroccan leather.

I felt the soft leather in my hands – still as impressive as I remembered it as a child. We all fell silent, words did not seem adequate or right at this moment, and I opened the Bible where the thin black ribbon invited me to read. When we read passages from the Bible, we come to it in a certain frame of mind, and as we read the words, God speaks to us, as we are. He speaks personally to each one of us. The Bible fell open at St Matthew's Gospel, Chapter 24, and immediately I read Verse 14. 'And this Gospel of the Kingdom shall be preached in all the world for a witness unto all nations; and then shall the end come'.

My Aunt spoke softly. 'It hasn't been opened since the day your grandmother died, and it was put away.'

I looked at the gold leaf edging still glowing in a wide band of enriching gold, and I looked at the fine italic script at the heading of each page.

I turned back to where the thin ribbon held open the pages at St Matthews Gospel and I read Verse 32. 'Now learn a parable of the fig tree. When his branch is yet tender and putteth forth leaves, ye know that summer is nigh'.

Summer was certainly nigh, it was at its height and the countryside was bathed in glorious sunshine, and the birds sang away to their hearts content.

De Quincy was right, with everything growing, the birds singing, death is hard to come to terms with. I thought back to my Sermon on St John's Gospel. 'I am the Vine, you are the branches'. When the branch has brought forth leaves in the fullness of Summer, so it brings the fruits of Autumn. I continued reading Verse 35 of St Matthew's Gospel open before me. 'Heaven and earth shall pass away but my words shall not pass away'. Verse 36, 'But of that day and hour knoweth no man, no not the angels of heaven but my Father only'. I closed the Bible and wondered if these were the last words my grandmother had read.

As we got up to leave, my Aunt smiled and leant forward. 'I know your grandmother wanted me to give you her Bible.' At that moment I looked intently at her and recognised the white curls around her round face and the bluey-grey eyes, and remembered the smile of the two old ladies, that bent over my bed. We said our farewells and I arrived back home deep in thought. I now recognised the two old ladies to be the two who had given me Bibles – the one in 1947, the other bought in 1927 but given to me in 1997. My Aunt had been the instrumental giver and her words and smile had told me who my guardian angels were. I smiled to think that angels were in the form of two old ladies. I always thought angels were cherubs as in Boticelli paintings, or as the Angel Gabriel with golden wings and halo. I wondered why I had not recognised my guardian angels until several weeks later when my Aunt, by the act of giving had opened my eyes. I thought of Jesus when he walked with two Disciples on the road to Emmaus. We were told in St Luke, Chapter 24, Verse 15, 'As they talked and discussed, Jesus himself drew near and walked along with them, they saw him but did not recognise him'. Jesus asked them why they were sad and his followers replied:

> Jesus was a prophet and was considered by God and by all the people to be powerful in everything he said and did. Our chief priests and rulers handed him over to be sentenced to death and he was crucified. This is the third day since it happened.
>
> Some women went at dawn to his tomb but could not find his body. They came back saying they had seen a vision of angels saying that he is alive.
>
> *Good News Bible*

It was only when Jesus and his two followers sat down to a meal together and Jesus leant forward and broke bread and gave a blessing that, 'Their eyes were opened and they recognised him, but he disappeared from their sight'.

I now had another piece of armour to add to my 1947 Bible, my cross and my card.

I settled down to sleep surrounded by my armour and thought how safe I felt – as safe as in my cell on Iona, when the Holy Spirit surrounded me and even the angel of death feared to look. The next morning I awoke early, roused by a persistent blackbird. It sang so sweetly and soulfully as though he regretted the departing summer, for today was the last day of August. As the sun rose golden on the distant hills, his song had had its fill. He sang of departing life as the sun rose and he would sing his same song as the sun set.

The shrill sound of the telephone stirred me into action and I wondered who could be ringing so early in the morning. It was Sunday and I was preaching and saying prayers at the early Communion Service. It was my daughter in America with the most terrible news that Diana, the Princess of Wales, had been killed in a car accident. She is eight hours behind us so had been awake at the time the incident was televised on American television. I received the news in stunned silence and disbelief, as I was too shocked to talk I said I would ring her later. I immediately set about altering my Sermon and Prayers and hurried off to church. I collected a paper which said Diana had been in an accident in Paris. As people came into church they were unaware of what had happened. They needed reassuring. If Diana, the Princess of Wales, could be taken in such a dramatic way; if the dream of beauty, promise, youthful love and hope could be removed at a stroke, what hope for the rest of the world? 'But of that day and hour knoweth no man'. (St Matthew Chapter 24, Verse 36.)

As we sang our hymns and read the Bible over the next few days, words jumped out to reassure and comfort. Old hymns seemed to take on new meaning as the world struggled to come to terms with its bereavement.

The hymn, 'In Heavenly Love Abiding', was to be heard on radio and television and the last line, 'And He will walk with me', left a deep impression. 'Breathe on me Breath of God', with its last line of, 'So shall I never die', became a great comfort.

Psalm 23, 'The Lord's my Shepherd', loved by all; and Psalm 46, 'God is always ready to help in times of trouble – even if the seas roar and rage, and the hills are shaken by the violence – The Lord Almighty is with us'. St Paul who quoted Jesus, 'I am the resurrection and the life.' And St Paul reassured us that nothing can separate us from God. St John who saw a New Heaven and a New Earth, a New Holy City, a New Jerusalem, and told us – Jesus will wipe away every tear, there will be no more death, no crying, no pain. And so we listened and became reassured, and no more land mines.

Finally, we listened to the well known hymn, 'The King of Love My Shepherd Is', with the last line, 'With thee dear Lord beside me'.

So the terrible day ended, and the numbness was replaced by action in the placing of flowers and the gathering of mourners to uphold each other, and the words of old but loved hymns stayed in our hearts.

And He will walk with me,
So shall I never die
With Thee Dear Lord beside Me

We moved on to Keats' 'Season of mists and mellow fruitfulness', and like Keats we ask, 'Where are the songs of Spring?' I thought back to that beautiful day in May at St Mary's when we looked for the signs of life. The watchful eyes of the mother bird as she sat on her nest, protecting the young. The fresh green buds, the wild flowers and the breeze; the promise of freedom and the coming of the Holy Spirit, and the assurance that the fruits would come.

Diana, Princess of Wales was to be buried at Althorpe, her family home, on 6th September. It was not to be a state funeral, but a 'special' funeral. On 5th September we heard that Mother Teresa had died, and this seemed to be a happy conclusion to a life of dedication and service. She was full of mercy rather than morals and when asked to comment on Aids patients in New York, where Aids patients were homosexuals, who had flaunted outrageous gay life styles, she responded, 'Love Them, Love Them, Love Them!' Diana, Princess of Wales reflected this opinion in her work for Aids and other charities, but both were about more than Charity work – even the Lottery supports charities. Both were saintly – one secular and one sacred. Saints as I had discovered in Iona, are very determined people who have a call to a higher purpose to serve.

The funeral of Diana, Princess of Wales, stopped the world for one minute's silence.

The funeral of Diana united the world for several minutes as the world said the Lord's Prayer – united, the world said, 'Our Father'.

The funeral touched the world, in the words of 'Candle in the Wind'.

As Earl Spencer said dramatically, 'Diana, Goddess of Hunting, was hunted.'

Elton John sang hopefully, 'Never fading with the sunset, when the rain set.'

Chapter Nine
Pilgrimage Continued

So as we moved into this season of mists, we might remember De Quincy. 'Slips into the noiseless deeps of the infinite, so sweet, so ghostly in its soft given smiles. Silent as a dream and quiet as the dying trance of a saint. Farewell to... farewell to Summer'.

I looked for my blackbird and awoke each morning hoping to hear his song. The mornings were becoming darker and the sun seemed reluctant to shine at its early hour as though in mourning. The fields seemed to cling to the morning mist in an attempt to hide. The flowers continued to pile up outside Kensington Palace, Althorpe, and monuments, and town halls. The world seemed to be on a pilgrimage clinging to flowers and hope, not knowing where they were going but looking for reassurance in an uncertain world of pain, crying, death and landmines. We were now well into September and the phone rang – it was my doctor at the hospital. He said I was to see him as soon as possible, so we arranged to meet that day! I did not ask any questions but wondered what could be so urgent to require the doctor himself to ring. I thought secretaries or nurses did this, and also, why the urgency? I was to meet him at Christies (Hospital) in Manchester, and as I drove the few miles, I wondered what was my fate? I didn't wait but was led into a cubicle where the doctor explained he had looked at the results of some tests and was not happy with the results. He told me I had had a large tumour, 2.5 cms removed and sixteen glands from under my arm, and the tablets he had previously prescribed did not appear to be effective.

'I am afraid you will need some more treatment. I am therefore recommending six months chemotherapy.' He asked me if I would be willing to begin that day, but when he realised I was on my own, he asked me to return the following day and start my treatment. I would be unable to drive myself to and from the hospital on that day.

It certainly seemed like an uncertain world, and yet hadn't I been told all this would happen? Hadn't I been warned of what lay ahead – how I would be afflicted, travailed and suffer, until that moment of despair when I watched myself get up; shrug, my shoulders and walk off; straight, calm, not a care in the world? I remembered how my body had been white with a translucent lightness; and complete aura of peace and light shone around and through me. How the Holy Spirit who had commanded me to 'watch and wait' and then protected me, had said, 'You shall not be overcome.'

Being a pilgrim was not easy, our day of pilgrimage in Iona proved that. The wind and rain watched our efforts as we struggled to reach St Columba's Bay, and as we held on to one another as we reached for our pebble. Then clutching our pebble the wind drove us back to the abbey, to a place of refuge. 'Pilgrimage is a journey through a vale of tears to a place of consolation' – a goal after a painful effort. If the dream is to be one of beauty, promise, love and hope we have to trust and then live the dream, act and lead. We have to be the dream, we the ordinary, the hopeless, the ugly even. If there is to be a dream we have to start and motivate the trail as the extraordinary become the every day ordinary. Whether the year is 1927, 1947 or 1997 until eternity – for we know not the hour.

5th September and Mother Teresa has died – 'such a death is a happy conclusion to a life,' and now on 6th September, Saturday, it was to be the funeral of Diana. The world watched and indeed it was not a 'happy conclusion to life.' What appeared to be a guarantee of security – marriage to a Prince with the world at her feet – was the opposite. What we plan and make out to be our ideal, our dream, is not to be. At times God appears not to hear us, not to answer our prayers but we only know in part, darkly as a reflection in a mirror. We need to lay down what is past and look to the future. We need to continue our journey, our pilgrimage, even if at times we are forced back by the wind. God has a plan, a wiser, more lasting plan than our transient dreams.

> The boast of heraldry, the pomp of power
> And all that beauty, all that wealth e'er gave,
> Awaits alike the inevitable hour,
> The paths of glory lead but to the grave[21]

September moved into October and as the sun shone on the golden beech, God would not allow melancholy. The horse chestnut spilled out its bounty – acorn and beech nuts lay thick and crunchy underfoot, red berries clung to every bush, there was the assurance of spring – that the fruits would come. The journey from spring to autumn was providing answers as our journey through life as pilgrims provides answers. There is always something worthwhile ahead, because the Lord is there already.

I searched out my pebble from Iona, the one I had collected from St Columba's Bay, when three of us had clung to each other for protection against the buffeting wind and driving rain. I felt the silky smoothness of its round shape and admired the soft sand, beige colour, with smudges of soft olive green, and veins of pure white and rust running through it. I felt recovery surge through my body, and with my pebble and the blue sky and the golden sun shining on the crisp leaves of the beech, I felt the storm had ceased.

> As, when a storm hath ceased, the birds regain,
> Their cheerfulness, and busily re-trim
> Their nests, or chant a gratulating hymn
> To the blue ether and bespangled plain;
> Even so, many a re-constructed fane,
> Have the survivors of this storm renewed
> Their holy rites with vocal gratitude:
> And solemn ceremonials they ordain
> To celebrate their great deliverance;
> Most feelingly instructed 'mid their fear –
> That persecution, blind with rage extreme,
> May not the less, through Heavens mild countenance,
> Even in her own despite both feed and cheer;
> For all things are less dreadful than they seem.[22]

This last line of Wordsworth's poem reminded me of the last line of Chaucer's poem. 'And trouthe thee shal deliver, it is no dred'. Poets often get inspiration from each other, and I wrote my own poem of recovery.

My eyes could now see clearly and my brain could understand the message. There were words on my blank sheet of paper. My vision had materialised, my tomorrow was clearer. God had sent me to Iona on a pilgrimage of the unknown but had revealed to me what lay ahead, and warned me and prepared me. Like a good teacher he had laid the facts before me and given me the armour I needed but I was the one to journey on. I had to continue my pilgrimage of discovery and however uncertain or hard the pilgrimage, whatever suffering or storms we might meet on our pilgrimage there is always something worthwhile ahead. A pilgrimage is not meant to be easy, our pilgrimage round the island on Iona proved that and we were blown back to begin again. However, a pilgrimage is a journey that provides answers, because the Lord has already gone before us and is there already waiting for us.

Recovery

I opened my eyes
And saw behind me the long dark tunnel
Through which I had passed.
The echoing silence was broken by the elated note of
    a soaring bird,
And my willing spirit soared too,
Grasping eagerly onto the trailing notes
Reviving with the effervescent freshness of freedom.
I embraced the free open spaces,
Serenaded by a wordless melody
And the unlimited view of paradise was mine.
I looked behind and sensed the presence of my outline,
Straight, unyielding, completely motionless,
And I in contrast relaxed as an aerated bubble
Moved effortlessly elated by emotion.
For its restriction held no bounds.
Recalled by a hidden voice:
My spirit stirred my stricken outline;
And touched my mind with that same tune,
To set a beat in my poetic pulse,
And with each trailing note of life
Leave words to fill that empty void.

Chapter Ten
The Gift of Sight

So the storm had ceased and my blackbird serenaded me every morning. He did not seem to notice it was no longer the middle of August, or even the middle of the day, and though the mornings gradually darkened and grew mistier and colder, he continued to sing the same song of life and birth. Autumn faded into winter that season of bare tree, bare soul, bereavement and death. I thought of Keats and his solitary hearth, 'when hateful thoughts unwrapped his soul in gloom, and no fair dreams before my mind's eye flit'.

I looked to my vision, the moment I had succumbed and fell unconscious only to shrug my shoulders, get up and walk away, strong, and renewed, full of new life. I constantly prayed and thanked God for the insight he had given me, and the protection. Whenever 'hateful thoughts unwrapped my soul', I returned to my cell in Iona, to my fortress where even the angel of death feared to look. Like my blackbird I was given the gift of sight, and could see through the mists to sunshine beyond. I remembered the words of George Macleod, 'It is a very thin place. There is only a thin separation between spirit and matter.' I remembered the tapes of Ron's stories I had brought back home, and settled in front of the fire to listen to his account of St Columba or Columcille.

I loved his stories of the Old Testament, and his stories of Jesus and by jotting down the title and a brief note, can recall the content of the stories, such as, 'Malachai' or 'Boaz' or 'Diane'. My journal would never end if I included a description of all these wonderful stories. However, I feel it is necessary and appropriate to recount, just the barest outline of Ron's story of St Columba.

Ron starts his story by telling us how St Columba would look out at the sea from his native Ireland. He could see through the mists to a distant island – like a jewel in the ocean. He watched the sea change from blue to green and saw it embrace the rocks and leave its warm puddles and pools of sparkling water. He watched the encircling gulls with their plaintive cry, and saw the roar of the pebbles pulled out by the tide. He saw the headlands and the moving corn as if ripples of sea. Columba had the gift of sight. He knew where a bird with a broken wing lay injured; and he knew one day he would have an island and a boat of his own. He would sit under the willow tree, a place of deep thought, and in his mind he saw the island and the boat.

His mother was visited by an angel who gave her a cloak of thistle down that sparkled with dew, and told her that the son she would give birth to would have the gift of sight and be called Columcille – Dove of the Church. His word would carry over the hills she saw and knew, and over the hills far away that she did not know and could not see. His mother knew Columba would go as directed, but she did not know where or when. Columba was sent to learn Latin and copy the Gospels and after this he was sent out with a staff in his hand, sandals on his feet, a bell to call people, and a Bible in his hand.

He went to Finian's Monastery where he built a hut or cell outside the church by the door. The description of this cell that Columba built reminded me very much of my room on Iona which was outside the main abbey; through the large abbey door and along the gravel path, I walked every night under the stars to my cell and over the door it said, the Abbot's house.

But to continue Ron's story... Finian showed Columba his treasure – a book like an angel with pictures, and letters in gold and red and green and blue. Columba thought he would copy the book so it could be shared. He worked every day and night to faithfully copy it and then when it was completed he fell asleep.

Finian was angry and said, 'This is my book.'

Columba said, 'This copy is my book for the people.' So they parted and a tribunal was held. It was decided that when a cow, belonging to a man, has a calf, the calf belongs to the cow, and so to the man, therefore the copy of the book belonged to Finian. A great disturbance broke out and Columba fled. He joined with people from the hills – bowmen and spearmen and won a great victory, but many were killed and Columba said, 'The death was bitter and the journey long,' and he grieved for what had happened. There was then a Church Tribunal and Columba was banished from Ireland – he was excommunicated.

Columba asked, 'How can I be banished from God who is so wonderful, so powerful?' However, he was banished from Ireland, so picked twelve strong men for their skills – a boat builder, a navigator, a farmer, a woodsman, a herdsman, etc. and he saw one weak man and picked him also because 'We will need someone to be kind to us.'

He set out in his boat and came to an island rising like a fortress out of the sea. He built a community, and each man built his own cell and from here they preached the Word.
The chief of the Druids came to visit and told Columba that Iona belonged to the Druids. Columba of course said, 'Iona belonged to God – the one in three.'

The chief Druid drew a circle round himself and said, 'Come no nearer,' and he left.

Columba continued to spread the word and came to a village made fearful by the Druids. He talked to them in the language they understood about food and about bread. He said, 'I come to talk to you about the bread of life. The seed dries and out of it comes the ear of corn, so in death there is life. When you take the ears of corn it is death to the ears, but bread and life to you.'

He told them about Jesus' death and how it means life to the world, and so their fear was gone. They brought their sons to be baptised in the well in the name of the One God, Father, Son and Holy Spirit. At one particular baptism a girl looked on and when Columba, tired, fell asleep, she came to the well. She told Columba her name was Deidre of the Sorrows. Columba said, 'The peace of Christ be with you,' and the girl ran off.

When visiting a village on the way to seek acquaintance with a king of the Picts he saw the girl and was told she was a slave to a Druid in Columba's home town. Columba went there to the depths of a cave lit by red fires as if lit with blood and asked for the release of the girl. The druid said no, so Columba said, 'Then you must die.'

'All men must die,' replied the Druid.

To which Columba said, 'But your death is just round the corner.' The Druid drew a circle round himself. Deidre managed to find Columba and tell him the boy who she had witnessed being baptised had had a curse put on him and he was dying. Columba went to the boy and held him to his heart and the boy began to breath, his eyelids fluttered, and his heart began to beat. The boy laughed and grief turned to joy. Columba set off again and the mists came down, but Columba of the 'seeing eye' found his way to the king of Druids.

However he was turned away. When Columba said, 'Let us in,' the king said, 'You are not welcome.'

Columba said, 'My God is all-powerful,' and he knocked

with his staff and entered the fortress where he preached his word. Columba left and on the way back stubbed his toe, bent down and picked up a pebble. Columba had the 'sight' and when several men caught up with them and said that the Druid king was dying, Columba said, 'Put this pebble on his chest and he will be healed.' However, Columba insisted that the Druid must release the girl slave Deidre. At the moment the Druid was healed the mist cleared and Deidre bounded over the heather – free.

Columba's ministry spread from Iona all over Scotland and down through England. Columba continued his special ministry from his special island, Iona, where he had arrived so many years earlier in his own boat.

Columba had the gift of sight and from Iona sent his seal of the Sacred Three: The seal of the God of Life, the seal of the Christ of Love, and the seal of the Spirit of peace and protection.

Chapter Eleven
The Shortest Day

It is December and I am over the half way mark in my chemotherapy treatment. It is now nearly six months since my operation and seven months since I was warned in a vision of what lay ahead. Everything in my vision has taken place with amazing accuracy, and all the time – every minute of my ordeals and trials – I feel under the protection of the Holy Spirit. I have tried to write down with similar accuracy these last seven months, since my pilgrimage to Iona. However, words seem inadequate to describe the unfolding of an amazing vision in which I walked under the protection of God.

We are fast approaching the shortest day. The mornings are dark and the evenings close in rapidly leaving only a few hours of pale sunshine. My blackbird sings only rarely – preferring the shelter of the bushes. However, his place has been taken by a cheeky robin whose song and bright red breast light up the grey subdued hours of these winter days. I recalled summer and the longest day and how I had drifted into peaceful sleep with the words of De Quincy drifting through my subconscious. 'Summer slips into the noiseless deeps of the infinite so sweet so ghostly in its soft golden smiles. Silent as a dream and quiet as the dying trance of a Saint.' (De Quincy, *Confessions of an English Opium Eater*).
Today is the shortest day and it came in silence as if a ghost...

and then was gone.

I got my shorthand notebook and wrote, 'The Captive' as a memory of this shortest day.

The Captive

The day displayed a beauty and a silence
With an icy stillness claimed by other winter days
Of ages long since melted with her snows.
Dark impenetrable yew trees with outer branches lit by clinging frost
Merged and huddled along a frozen gleaming pond,
Casting dark protective shadows where the frost could not reach.
Here defiant ripples escaped to nudge and smooth the glassy edge
Offering an oasis for ducks, with stiffly folded wings,
To pivot with a restricted air.
The fields beyond spread snow-bound to the snow-filled sky
From where gulls fell, to land upon the frozen pond
Like ghosts, their heads held upon a wing.
Winter's shortest day held between a frozen sky and frost-bound land.
A captive tightly clasped by a shadowy hand.
A mere phantom of the Spring-filled day,
And yet it was a moment's pause
As fleeting as the falling flakes
That melted as they fluttered down.
The day that came in silence as if a ghost, was gone.

One single beam escaped the sky
In rush of wings the ghosts were gone
The call of rooks pierced the silent air
That transient winter day, the shortest, was no longer there.
Like other winter days long since melted with the snow
One fleeting second had let her captive go.

On my calendar of Saints Days, it said the 21st of December was St Thomas' Day. Apart from St Thomas the disciple of Jesus, there was Thomas Becket and Thomas Aquinas – all saints.

Thomas Aquinas was born in 1225 and his life was devoted to teaching and writing. He wrote a *Summa Theoloica*, a great theological work which was translated into twenty-two volumes but he never finished his work. He wrote the following words:

> All I have written seems to me like so much straw with what I have seen and with what has been revealed to me.

This seemed to put into words exactly how I felt.

Chapter Twelve

Adieu! And Forward to the Dawn

So the transient winter days slipped by. Hardly was it dawn when dusk appeared but winter evenings bring a strange, silent kind of excitement and sometimes I would wrap up and slip down the 'Valley' and wander along with the stream, and the night. Tonight, the night of the 22nd of December, there was a hush and serenity, and the tiniest sliver of a new moon shone above. I wandered along the Ladybrook Stream, in the valley at the back of my house and felt in communion with nature. It seemed a long time since I had been able to walk freely like this – so much had happened since the spring and my communion with the Saints on Iona. It seemed such a long time since my quiet day at St Mary's, Alderley, when the signs of spring were all around. I walked back to the road and under the light from the street lamp, I got out my shorthand notebook and pen, and rested against the roots of a huge beech tree to write. As I wrote, the new moon began to sink and I sensed complete solitude, and yet I sensed a spirit, a friendly presence that came face to face as though reconciling me with past events. I seemed to write for hours and suddenly realised it was dark, dark and cold. I hurriedly penned in the last line and titled these rambling thoughts, 'Face to Face'.

Face to Face

When the night with serenity had fallen
And all the creatures in their twos departed,
I, accompanied by the newest moon
That meekly shone with unaccustomed glow,
Wandered to a haven, that many times
Welcomed me with soothing open arms.
A place of quiet retreat, away from crowds,
In communion with nature, with privacy deep.
In seclusion of oaks, and beech and fir.
A dwelling, no careless onlooker would seek
Or happen upon, but fitted to the ground
From whence it sprang, and quietly sheltered
By sweet, silent overgrowth of wild flowers.
Along the trackless paths, led by a sense
Of belonging, the sweet night air
Guided my steps to the unobtrusive door,
Subdued, and unseen in approach.
Silver beams outlined the wild rose,
Honeysuckle, and brambles wayward growing there
Each with the other like spirits in repose.
How long, I fear to say, since I had felt
The woodland grass beneath my feet
The wild flowers, the fallen thorn,
Wild with Nature, in all her freedom

Strewn about in carefree happiness
In this natural haven of sweet retreat.
All night the moon shone on and on...
And never stopped until supreme
It reigned above this wild abode,
And gazed in wonder through the willow trees
Casting reflections into a slumbering pond.
No calmer place to rest and dream
And merge with thoughts beyond
What had, and might have been.
I stood in hazy recollection of this spot
Remembering the sleepy hedgehog that happened along:
A visitor in a moment's interlude.
The leafy bowers of dappled sunlight;
A resting place for head and heart,
And birds to sing a fleeting song.
The sweet night air dropped in dew,
For now the moon is on the wane
And left an overpowering solitude:
A sudden moment of mystery,
In which no light penetrated through,
And groping in this darkened place
I felt and sensed soul giving inspiration
As though I with a spirit, face to face
Were meeting with the past again.
Not facts, or anything to feel and see,

Or happenings controlled by time,
Not of the senses is the memory.
Far deeper does the mystery lie
So many thoughts that flow through me
But only one, love it is that cannot die.

The hush and serenity of the 22nd December brought the first wintry showers. Following this strangely calm night fell those first snows of winter. I awoke on the 23rd to a light flurry of snow, but it was dry and clung to every twig, and blade of grass and lit up the world into a magical winter wonderland. It was strangely silent and I wondered if perhaps we would have a truly Dickensian white Christmas for surely, 'Not a creature stirred.' My blackbird was nowhere to be seen, but a robin stared fixedly at me from a branch of the apple tree. He fluffed his feathers out against the bitter cold air and cocked his head on one side. I could not resist his appeal and went to see if I had any nuts or crumbs that I could put on the hedge for him. Robins are not gregarious birds and he seemed lonely in this snow-laden landscape, devoid of any other bird or creature.

The Robin

Leave this bare and half-stripped scene;
Fly down from off your snowy perch;
Leave that laden, winter-captured tree.
'Come and be a friend to me.'

> The withered plant obeys the call,
> Is silenced by the soft white fall.
> 'But come and be a friend to me,'
> As you and I are meant to be.
>
> The other birds have flown their nest,
> But you dear robin look your best
> On snowbound earth where we are free.
> 'Fly down and be a friend to me.'
>
> The sun obeys, is forced to sink,
> The pond is stilled, but see, I offer drink,
> And scatter on the ground some bread
> For you gay bird, fluffed out in red.
> The snow fell thick and fast all night,
> When dawn appeared concealed in white:
> He rent the air with piteous plea,
> 'Come out and be a friend to me'.

By the 23rd the snow had gone but it was bitterly cold with a sharp wind blowing from the East. I was kept indoors, and put on a tape of Celtic music – surrounded myself with memories of Iona: my wave-worn pebbles, postcards, candle snuffers and photographs of the abbey and friends. Feeling the smoothness of my special pebble, the one I had braved the wind with, and lashing rain, on my pilgrimage round the island of Iona, and which I had collected from St Columba's Bay. I closed my eyes, listened to the harp, and was transported back to the abbey.

Many times have I thought back to my vision. Was I awake at least for part of the vision, and if so when did I fall asleep? When was I put into that terrible dream of temptation, travail and infliction? Had I in fact left my body and become an observer – because how else could I watch my body rise from unconsciousness and walk away with a shrug of the shoulders, into light and peace. I am convinced I was awake and saw with my own eyes the direct, swift descent of the angel of death over my room – with sure intent on claiming me. With the same certainty I know the Holy Spirit stood over the door so no harm could come to me, and I heard the authoritative command of, 'watch and wait,' three times. I dread to think of what would have become of me if I had left my room to investigate the agonised screams. I felt the presence from the door fill the room until it was all around me so that my cell was secure and safe. I felt the awfulness of the danger, and whilst my heart pounded against my chest I knew I was protected by God and was completely and utterly safe and calm.

Memories of Iona easily flooded back as I listened to the harp playing Celtic songs and tunes – some we had learned to sing during a 'Wee Sing' in the abbey on the Friday afternoon as dusk fell. We had also gathered in the cloisters, parts of which dated back a thousand years, to sing with the 'Spirit Singers' from Canada. We arranged ourselves on the square of grass enclosed on all sides by the quadrangle of ancient arches. Inside these arches along where the saints of Columba's early Christian community would walk, it was dark, sombre and prayerful, but out in the quadrangle on the grass the stone walls of the abbey rose to greet a pure blue sky. Shafts of clear April sunshine beamed down on our gathering, welcomed our voices turned upwards in song and, gathering our Celtic strains, released the music out into the open and over the seas. Something about the sheer freedom of singing in the open and letting our voices float upwards to the blue sky reminded me of my blackbird and the robin and the delightful freedom of the birds as they serenade the seasons.

Thoughts of Spring

How perennial the seasons are,
Their beauty of eternal art
Beats together with my heart.
The thrush who fills the early dawn,
The blackbird with his farewell call,
'The owlet's wing that brushed the lawn,
The robin in mid winter from his snow-topped wall,
Plucks my heartstrings yet again,
Sweet fleeting notes from Celtic harp,
'Come Holy Spirit' of the everlasting strain.

I thought about our meditation on the Monday morning – the world was receding, as we had been in the abbey two days now. Our world was one of blue skies, reflected blue seas, lambs and saints. In our meditation we thought about the 'stepping stones' that led us to Iona. We wrote down the five people who had influenced us most as we took our faltering steps forward to faith. I was surprised to see William Wordsworth headed my list of five people with the greatest influence, and I was intrigued to realise I had followed closely in the direction he had taken. We had many fateful facts in common, not least that we had lost both our parents early in life and had a close bond with a sister. All facts outside our control. The second person who influenced my early steps in faith was my maternal grandmother, who had the time to read the Bible to me as I sat at her feet. She died when I was fifteen years old and stayed in my subconscious, with precious memories of her Bible locked away in my mind. Again I was surprised to see I had written her name as second of the five people in my list. This unlocking of my mind and turning to the people who had led me forward in faith was to result in amazing occurrences over the following months. Not least the meeting, after many years, with my mother's sister – the only remaining child of my grandmother. The amazing fact of realisation of who my guardian angels were as my Aunt leant forward, and gave me my grandmother's Bible. I had not set eyes on this Bible since my grandmother had died, and how my Aunt thought to give it to me when she has three children of her own and eight grandchildren, and many great-grandchildren can only be a part of my guardian angel's plan. On the third morning of my sighting of the two old ladies, they smiled and said, 'She is all right now,' as though their deed was accomplished. It was several weeks later when I recognised who the old ladies were.

So there were three other people on my list of five but these three are not connected with this vision and story of Iona, but they are equally valuable stepping stones in my life. They belong to another vision and another story of pilgrimage.

It is Christmas Eve, the world is throbbing with activity – there is mass exodus as people flee from one place to another. We can see the planes taking off in all directions from the airport nearby. They leave vapour trails pouring north, south, east and west, as some leave for a sunny climate and some return for a winter Christmas.

We have not had a white Christmas for many years. My youngest child is fifteen years old and he has never seen a white Christmas. However, 1982, the year he was born, we were snowbound from late October to March and I wrote the 'Spirit of Winter'. Here are three verses from that poem.

Spirit of Winter

Deep Winter breathes in stillness through the wood.
In icy droplets decorating the deadened twig.
In clinging stars that glisten in the hedgerows,
And icicles that hang and pierce the frozen pond.
A scene deserted and untouched by humanity,
Hushed and softly yielding to the Heavens
In purity and beauty, and to what unseen wonders
Do nature and this season belong?

Deep winter sighs with stillness through the wood
Softly shaped in shades of peaceful solitude,
Clinging quietly in nooks and crevices
Of hushed calm, white and deep
As if abandoned to an everlasting sleep.
Earth and Sky, softly white between
A winter stillness, so beautiful
With a presence and a spirit both unseen.

Deep winter lies in silence in the wood,
Yet far away through laden trees
A rushing stream is heard, and small and low
Descends a winter sun with crimson glow.
As night descends, a tuneful bird
Flings his soul upon the snow
And through the silence of the wood
All harmonies are one.

As I watched the winter sun descend – slipping in and out of the darkening clouds to disappear in a trail of red vapour – I reminisced on the disappearing months and how they had slipped in and out between dusk and dawn, darkness and light. As I read the last lines of my poem written years ago, my blackbird sang and flung his soul upon the scene.

I awoke with a start as though someone had broken dawn's silence with a gun blast, and I sat bolt upright – it was Christmas Day. I rushed to the window like a child and saw that the sun was struggling behind the hill with Bowstones Farm glowing pink, as the sun struggled to emerge and light the sky. I looked to the distant Derbyshire hills and saw how quickly they responded to the dawn and became visible and grew nearer by the minute. It came to me how, as the world waits for Christmas Day to dawn and as I wait for the sun to rise, the world is looking to the year 2000. How quickly it is coming – it will soon be 1998 and in one year we will be waiting for the dawn to rise to celebrate the 2000th year of the coming of Light into the World.

I wondered how quickly the world will respond to this dawn, and become visible – for when Jesus brings his Light he will light up the world – for where he is there can be no darkness.

Christmas Day was spent in complete happiness – my daughter, unknown to me, had flown in from America and so the family was complete. As the sun had lit up the day sky, so the stars lit up the night sky. It had been a beautiful day and the evening seemed too beautiful to be of the earth.

The Evening is too Beautiful

The evening is too beautiful to be of the earth.
It is a beauty of the mind, not of the sense,
Of the soul, it is part of the Heavens.
Too remote to be felt by the pulsating heart.
A star sheds its light to the earth
But the source is in the Heavens.
Like a shadow cast to the ground from above,
The light and the shadow exist only as part of the earth.
But the source can rise and move in freedom,
For it is not chained, as the human body is chained.
But that tiny spark called soul from which the human is cast
Is like the star – it is in the Heavens,
And ultimately controls the actions of its immense part below:
For the light it sheds covers a greater distance than the star itself.
The star is an all powerful source of energy
And the light it casts feeble in its immensity.

And the light is subject to day and night
To the year, the hour, the second
But the star is not aged as the self is aged, nor subject to the second.
Your soul is in Heaven:
The immortal spark of your very being;
That part of your mortal self which is linked by love.

The star is the soul, love is the beam,
The light it casts is the frail mortal being that is you.
Therefore you are shed to the earth in love,
And recalled in love.
For your immense part is of the earth,
But your greater part is of the Heavens.
Will you now, you frail mortal being, fear death?

The following days slipped by and into the 31st of December and New Year's Eve. We were invited to celebrate with neighbours and as Big Ben chimed midnight we raised our glasses of champagne to health and happiness in 1998. Before falling asleep I gathered my armour around me – the lopsided cross, the card with a lamb in Jesus' hands, my two Bibles from my guardian angels and I placed my smooth pebble from Iona on my chest so I might be healed.

> 'Protect me O God, I trust in you for safety:
> I say to the Lord, 'You are my Lord, all the good things
>   I have come from you.'
> 'You Lord, are all I have, and you give me all I need,
>   my future is in your hands.'
> I am always aware of the Lord's presence;
> He is near, and nothing can shake me.
>
>
> I am so thankful and glad, and I feel completely
>   secure.
> Because you protect me from the power of death.
> 'You will show me the path that leads to life,
> Your presence fills me with joy and brings me plea-
>   sure for ever.'
>
>   Psalm 16, from the *Good News Bible*

I fell asleep.

Adieu! adieu! Thy plaintive anthem fades;
Past the near meadows, over the still stream,
Up the hill-side, and now 'tis buried deep.
In the next valley-glades:
Was it a vision, or a waking dream?
Fled is that music... do I wake or sleep?[23]

Notes to the Text

[1] *Community Workshop Book*

[2] Wordsworth, W., untitled poem taken from *Poems referring to the Period of Childhood*. Ref: Deselincourt, Earnest, *Wordsworth Poetical Works A New Edition*, Oxford University Press, Reprinted 1973.

[3] *Iona Service Book*

[4] 'Iona upon Landing', by W. Wordsworth. Ref: Deselincourt, Earnest, *Wordsworth Poetical Works A New Edition*, Oxford University Press, Reprinted 1973.

[5] 'The Prelude', by William Wordsworth

[6] 'Iona', by W. Wordsworth. Ref: Deselincourt, Earnest, *Wordsworth Poetical Works A New Edition*, Oxford University Press, Reprinted 1973.

[7] Introduction to 'The Prelude', by W. Wordsworth.

[8] Part of the Prelude 'Schooltime', by W. Wordsworth. Ref: Deselincourt, Earnest, *Wordsworth Poetical Works A New Edition*, Oxford University Press, Reprinted 1973.

[9] *Iona Worship Book*.

[10] 'Devotional Incitements', by W. Wordsworth. Ref: Deselincourt, Earnest, *Wordsworth Poetical Works A New Edition*, Oxford University Press, Reprinted 1973.

[11] *Iona Service Book*.

[12] *Iona Service Book*.

[13] Preface to the second edition under the title of 'Lyrical Ballads', Ref: DeSelincourt, Earnest, *Wordsworth Poetical Works A New Edition*, Oxford University Press, Reprinted 1973.

[14] From 'We are Seven', by William Wordsworth.

[15] Wordsworth, W., untitled poem taken from *Poems referring to the Period of Childhood*. Ref: Deselincourt, Earnest, *Wordsworth Poetical Works A New Edition*, Oxford University Press, Reprinted 1973.

[16] From 'Elegy Written in a Country Churchyard' by Thomas Gray

[17] From 'To Hope', by John Keats.

[18] 'Cornish Cliffs' from *High and Low*, by John Betjeman, 1966.

[19] From *Confessions of an Opium Eater*.
[20] From *Confessions of an English Opium Eater*, by Thomas De Quincey.
[21] From Elegy written in a Country Churchyard by Thomas Gray.
[22] 'Recovery' by William Wordsworth.
[23] From 'The Nightingale' by John Keats.